"How do we do this?" Jo asked, kneeling before Maggie's electric recliner. "We weren't very successful last time."

"Maybe we have to want it bad enough to be ingenious," Maggie replied, sucking air when Jo slid a hand up the leg of her shorts. "Kiss me."

Jo tore off her suit jacket, removed her skirt and panties and kneeled on the chair. She whispered into Maggie's mouth, "God, you're wet."

Maggie breathed back, "Doesn't it feel good? I'm not going to last long." Then, "Are the doors locked?"

"I don't know and I don't care." She strained against Maggie's hand.

The cast cut at Maggie's armpit, curbing her passion. Jo's muscles closed on her hand as her fingers slid inside on a river of desire. Pulling them out slowly, she teased with long, slow strokes. "You are so swollen."

Jo thrust her tongue into Maggie's mouth and plunged her fingers deep inside. When she withdrew them, she began a tantalizing finger dance.

They were both moving now toward climax. It came simultaneously, something they seldom managed under even the best circumstances.

About the Author

Jackie Calhoun is the author of *Lifestyles, Second Chance, Sticks and Stones, Friends and Lovers* and *Triple Exposure*. She has had stories in *The Erotic Naiad, The Romantic Naiad* and *The First Time Ever*. She lives with her other half in the Wisconsin she loves and writes about.

CHANGES

by
JACKIE CALHOUN

THE NAIAD PRESS, INC.
1995

Printed in the United States of America on acid-free paper
First Edition

Editor: Christine Cassidy
Cover designer: Bonnie Liss (Phoenix Graphics)
Typesetter: Sandi Stancil

Library of Congress Cataloging-in-Publication Data

Calhoun, Jackie.
   Changes / by Jackie Calhoun.
      p.   cm.
   ISBN 1-56280-083-3 (pbk.)
   1. Lesbians—Middle West—Fiction.   I. Title.
PS3553.A3985C43   1995
813'.54—dc20   95-14532
                                          CIP

To my support group.
With thanks.

Some of the locations in this book are actual places, but the characters and story are fiction.

I

Peering up from under her brows, Maggie watched the two joggers change course. She heard the thudding of their running shoes on the road's surface, their harsh breathing as they approached. All other sounds had stopped.

She didn't wonder at this complete change in focus. Only minutes ago she'd been speeding through sunlight shafted by pine trees, listening to the rasping of her own breath, the clicking of the bicycle chain, the sound of tires on the pavement, the raucous cawing of crows nearby. She'd been thinking about Wisconsin summers — long-awaited, too brief and therefore intensely enjoyed.

To her left a thick stream of blood flowed slowly away from where her forehead was ground into the blacktop. It reminded her of lava moving down a volcano. She didn't want to think about how badly her neck ached, the lack of feeling in her arms and hands.

The woman jogger squatted beside her. "Take it easy. We'll get help."

"Don't move me. Please," she said.

Dripping sweat, the male runner stood behind his companion for the space of a minute, then said, "I'll go call for an ambulance."

She listened to him jog away. It would take an ambulance at least half an hour to reach her. Knowing she shouldn't change position, but unable to stand the discomfort, she made a decision. "I have to turn on my back." As her arms flopped to her sides, her fingers tingled.

Looking into startlingly light blue eyes, she noticed the color warming as the laugh-lines deepened and the woman smiled.

"My name's Erica Young. Do you live near here?" The woman's voice shook.

Maggie breathed a little easier, thinking here was someone who would take care of her. "We're renting a cottage on Pheasant Lake but no one's there." Certainly not Jo, who had left that morning for Oshkosh. She attempted a smile, even as she noticed a middle-aged woman standing nearby with one hand clapped over her mouth. Had she been there before? She didn't think so. But there were other sounds now — cars, voices, footsteps.

Another woman of indeterminate age knelt next to her, across from Erica, and explained a little breathlessly, "I'm a first responder. What's your name?"

"Maggie Saunders."

"Maggie, I need to put this cervical immobilization device on you. Okay? Just as a safety measure."

The device, a huge collar, prevented her from turning her head and cut off whatever peripheral vision she'd had. The sky reminded her of Erica's eyes, which she could no longer see. Staring at puffy white clouds moving overhead, she wondered what time it was. She'd begun her ride around eight-thirty that morning, had ridden maybe half an hour before the accident. It was probably a little after nine. Silently calculating, she figured that once the ambulance reached her it might take another half-hour to get her off the pavement and to the nearest hospital. An hour of waiting.

At the moment of impact, she had thought she was being punished. For what? For turning Bill and the kids' lives upside down after sixteen years of marriage so that she could fulfill her own selfish needs? But that was three years ago. For being a lesbian? She had argued with Jo that morning, who had teamed up with her ex-lover for racquetball and tennis and softball. Why should she be jealous of the time Jo spent with Gail when she herself didn't go in for those sports? Instead she was a solitary biker, and look where that had led her.

The other runner returned. He stood uncertainly behind Erica, who held her hand. She found herself clinging to this woman as if she were a lifeline, especially after the first responder asked her if she could feel her fingers, her toes. The responder, whose name escaped her even as she introduced herself, had tapped her extremities before asking, "Can you feel your hands, your feet?"

The implication of the question, which the woman continued to ask every few minutes, began to frighten her. *Don't let me be paralyzed. Please.* Sheepishly, she realized she was begging to a god she no longer believed existed. What gave her the right to ask favors? Apparently, her faith hadn't been expunged. It lurked there, surfacing when there was a crisis. If she were God, she would be tempted to ignore such appeals. They were akin to going to church only at Easter and Christmas.

The rise and fall of the siren jolted her into the moment. It occurred to her that neither her friends nor her family knew of her condition. Why had she let the bicycle headlight vibrate loose? Why hadn't she grabbed for it before it hung dangling by its wires from the handlebars? She wasn't sure exactly what had happened, but she knew somehow the light had stopped the bicycle, and she'd been propelled like a missile toward the road's surface. And it had all happened so fast that she couldn't recall the actual fall.

She'd done it this time, she thought, looking into the brown eyes of an emergency medical technician. Her carelessness had caught up with her but good.

He spoke in a loud voice as if she were old, hard of hearing or both. "We're going to put you on a board and fasten your head to it. It's a protective measure, to immobilize your neck and head. Then we'll load you into the ambulance. Okay?"

Unable to nod, she gave him a shaky smile and reluctantly let go of Erica's hand.

He took her fingers in his and asked the questions she dreaded. "Can you feel your fingers?" He grasped her foot. "Your toes?"

"Yes." She panicked now, sure that at any minute all feeling would be gone. Again she began to plead silently. *Let me die instead. Please. Don't let me be paralyzed.* She tried bargaining. *I'll do anything. I'll give more to charity. I'll even go to church every Sunday.* Would she give up Jo? It was no use. Any god worth her or his salt would recognize the promises as lies.

On the count of three the EMTs lifted her onto the board, strapped her head to it, and on another number three slid the board into the back of the rescue wagon. Erica wished her luck, promising to visit.

The ceiling of the van rocked overhead. Occasionally, the EMT next to her leaned forward enough for her to see her face. Maggie clung to her hand as she had to Erica's. How unlike her to need physical contact with a stranger. Several times the woman touched her hands and feet and asked the questions that frightened her so. A blood-pressure sleeve had been attached to her upper arm and closed with timed frequency like an unseen hand.

At the hospital, still fastened to the board, she was wheeled along white-ceilinged halls on a gurney — her view restricted to what was directly within her tunneled vision. Sounds took on new meaning. She overheard snatches of conversation, mostly pertaining to herself and her condition. Faces leaned over her, hands touched her. She gleaned a little comfort from the contact, unless or until it was followed by the inevitable questions.

After X-rays, she was wheeled back to emergency where the doctor's disembodied face hovered over her. He spoke in fractured English. "The X-rays show your neck broken. We must send you to hospital in Neenah where there is neurosurgeon. Theda Clark Medical Center is one of best hospitals in Wisconsin, in country." His face disappeared from view. "Cover the head wound," he said to some unseen person.

My neck is broken. Had she suspected that? She had known she shouldn't move from the moment of impact, but she had refused to believe it.

"Who can we contact? Do you have relatives at home or nearby or a friend you'd like us to notify?" an invisible presence asked.

Rather than define Jo as her lover, her partner, her roommate, she said, "The people who own the cottage we were renting, the Paynters." Harriet and Donald would tell Jo, who would inform her family and everyone else who needed to know.

She heard discussion concerning the Theda Star, the Theda Clark Medical Center helicopter. But then the gurney once again rolled over smooth floors, doors opened and shut, and she was lifted into the ambulance. Unseen voices surrounded her.

My neck is broken. She recalled a young boy who had fractured his neck in a diving accident, rendering him quadriplegic. Recently, there had been a collision and the driver of one of the cars had died instantly from a broken neck. Broken necks were equated with paralysis and/or death. No one got off scot-free.

The EMTs climbed back into the rescue wagon with her and reattached the blood-pressure cuff. She clutched the hand of the woman EMT who again sat next to her, whose face drifted in and out of her vision but whose voice soothed her.

"We'll take the main roads to Neenah. There won't be so many turns or hills. And we'll warn you before we turn on the siren, when we pass or need the right-of-way."

She knew the route, knew exactly where they were at each turn and intersection. State Highway 22 to Wautoma, Highway 21 to US 41, 41 north to Neenah. She took comfort confirming their location with the EMT, because it positioned her time-wise. She checked off an approximate time of destination against their whereabouts — less than an hour left, then a half-hour, fifteen minutes, a few minutes. When they reached the hospital, she reasoned she would be able to get off the board and would receive some pain medication. Her neck and head throbbed, her back ached.

Resolutely, she banished her present condition from her thoughts and let her mind roam to more pleasant matters, which was how she usually managed pain and misery. She envisioned Jo with her summer tan, the tips of her short brown curls bleached by the sun, freckles scattered across her nose and cheeks. She smiled, then remembered her parting words, thrown with stupid carelessness at Jo's departing back: "Why don't you just spend the night with her too?" God, if she'd only known, but she had a sneaking suspicion that even knowing wouldn't have mattered.

After what seemed hours, they crossed the bridge over the river and pulled into Theda Clark's E.R. The doors opened, the gurney was unloaded. Again she stared at white ceilings moving in line with her vision. Thinking that this could get very boring, she was glad that the worst would soon be over. They would no doubt get her off the torturous board, give her a shot or hook her up to one of those morphine-dispensing machines.

X-rays first, always. Forty-five agonizing minutes passed while the scanner studied her neck centimeter by centimeter and she held the attendant's hand. Then she was returned to E.R., where she once more gazed at the white tiles overhead. What time was it? She asked the attendant.

"One o'clock." He came to her side and squeezed her hand. "How are you doing?"

She shifted her lower half as she had been doing since she got here. "My back hurts. When can I get off this board?"

"When the neurosurgeon comes. He's in surgery. We can't chance taking you off the board because of your neck. Too much of a risk."

"Yes," she said in a small voice. Just her luck. What had been the point of speeding her here if she was only to be kept waiting. Where was Jo? Still at her parents'? With Gail? She hadn't been able to remember either Gail's number or the elder McCooks'.

"Let's put pillows under your back and knees. Maybe they'll help."

"Thanks," she said gratefully. It did ease some of

the strain. She could hear him moving quietly around the room. And when she couldn't hear him, she asked, "Are you there?"

"Right here." He came over to hold her hand for a few moments.

A kind man, but she was beginning to feel abandoned. When the shift changed and another attendant took over, she asked if anyone had inquired about her.

"There's someone out there who's been asking for you."

Her heart leaped. It had to be Jo. "Can she come in here?"

"Sure."

Why hadn't anyone told her she had a visitor? She felt indignant.

"How are you, sweetie?" Jo gave her a shaky smile and bent to kiss her. She took her hand in both of hers.

She didn't know until that moment how much she had wanted to be with Jo, had needed to see her. She clung to her hand. "How did you know I was here?" she asked, feeling somehow safer.

"I called the Paynters to ask you to call. I felt bad about the way we left each other this morning."

"Well, then maybe there was a reason for our fight. You never would have called otherwise."

"How do you feel?"

"My back, my neck, my head are killing me. I've got to get off this board."

"What's that thing around your neck?"

"I can't remember what it's called. Are you all

9

right? You look kind of sick, Jo." Jo's freckles stood out against the pallor under her tan. Her pupils nearly blotted the gray out of her eyes.

"I'm fine. I just need to sit down, is all." But when Jo sat, Maggie couldn't see her.

"Why is your forehead bleeding?"

She touched the gauze that covered the wound. Her fingers slid in gooey dampness. She felt the nurse peel off the covering, then quickly replace it.

"Someone needs to stitch that," Jo insisted, suddenly standing beside her.

When the nurse went off, presumably to call a doctor, Maggie whispered conspiratorially, "Good thing you're here." Relieved, she gave her care over to Jo's vigilant concern.

"You'll be all right, sweetie," Jo assured her, squeezing her hand.

"Do you think you should call me sweetie? Someone might catch on." After all, it was Jo who worried about the professional ramifications of being uncloseted.

"I love you."

"Shhh. I love you too," she murmured.

"A doctor will be here soon to take care of the wound," someone said from close by.

Had the attendant heard them?

"You'll be just like new then," Jo said with a brave smile.

The words, meant to comfort, made her realize with sinking hopes that no one else had told her she was going to be okay. "I'm not all right, Jo. My neck is broken."

"What?" Jo sat down suddenly, disappearing from her sight. "She said her neck is broken."

"It is," the attendant replied.

Silence. Then Jo spoke in a voice she barely recognized. "I'll be right back. I have to use the bathroom."

"Hurry."

A while later, her head stitched, herself catheterized, awaiting the neurosurgeon with Jo once more at her side, she signed the papers admitting herself to the hospital.

"Lucky I'm conscious," she remarked.

"We're partners," Jo muttered after the woman from admittance left, "and I can't be responsible for you. We share everything, but we have no legal rights."

"Well, it wouldn't matter if you were a man. If we weren't married, you still couldn't sign for me."

"Yes, but then we could at least choose to marry."

Pushing through the door and into their presence, the neurosurgeon loomed over them — a tall, lean, dark man. "Hi. Your name is Maggie?" He glanced at her chart. "I'm Dr. Hartland. This is my nurse, Jennifer. I'm sorry you had to wait. I was in surgery."

Actually, she had been waiting without painkillers, fastened to the board, something like seven or eight hours. Thinking this was the person who would end her ordeal, she gave him a grateful smile.

"You ever heard of a halo?" He was looking at her X-rays, holding one up to the light. "Not the kind the angels wear, but the type we put on people with broken necks to allow them mobility."

"No," she said and almost added that she didn't care. "When can I get off this board?" What she wanted was a soft bed.

"As soon as the halo is on and we have some traction exerted on your neck. What happened anyway?"

"I was thrown off my bike."

"Unsafe at any speed, huh?" He explained the procedure, that he would put four screws into her head to hold the halo in place. Then he turned to Jo. "It might be best if you wait outside, if you're at all queasy. We'll take good care of her." He smiled and winked at Maggie.

As she felt the pressure and heard the crunching, she thought, how medieval, how barbaric. Dr. Hartland was screwing screws through her anesthetized skin and into her skull. He then attached weight to the halo for temporary traction. An intravenous needle was inserted in her hand so that electrolytes and pain medication could be dispensed through it.

At five-thirty she was transferred from the board to a bed and wheeled to a hospital room.

II

"Where've you been, Jo?" Maggie asked.

"I phoned Nancy and Liz. They're on their way. How do you feel?"

"Better, sleepy. Did you call Kat? She can tell my kids."

Her son and daughter lived in Milwaukee. Three years ago, when she had separated from Bill, she'd taken their two children with her. Shelley was fifteen at the time, Mike twelve. Last year, when Maggie moved into Jo's house, Mike returned to his father's home, and Shelley moved in with her Aunt Katherine and Katherine's lover, Paul. It still hurt to remember that time, and she wondered briefly how Kat and the kids would react. They hadn't been pleased with the changes in her life since she left Bill.

"Not yet. I'll do it soon."

"Tell her not to alarm them, Jo. I don't want anyone thinking they have to rush here. Oh, and I need my insurance card out of my purse. Someone has to inform the insurance company of where I am and why, or they won't pay." Talking exhausted her.

"Maybe Liz or Nancy can find time to go to the lake and get your purse and pack our stuff," Jo said. "Or the Paynters would probably be glad to do it."

Maggie didn't care who did it. She and Jo wouldn't be going back to the cottage to finish their two weeks of vacation. Giving herself over to sleep, she awoke with a start when Jo, who was holding her hand, jumped.

Nancy and Liz were standing next to the bed, their faces twin expressions of wrinkled concern.

"Hi, you two. What happened?" Nancy said.

"You tell them, Jo."

"I don't know exactly what happened, only that it was a bicycle accident and Maggie's neck is broken. I thought there was just that wound on her forehead. She had to tell me herself." Jo sounded angry. "I couldn't even sign the admittance forms. We would have had to get Shelley to do that if Maggie hadn't been able to."

"Want to walk down to the end of the hall, Jo?" Nancy said, glancing at Liz. "There's a lounge overlooking the river."

"Let's go down to the lobby. I need to call Katherine."

Liz said, "I'll keep Maggie company."

Night closed in on Maggie when Jo left. She couldn't turn her head, so the room remained a place of shadows. People had to walk into her direct line of vision to be seen. She clutched the control to the morphine-dispensing machine that stood next to her bed. It only dispersed medication at timed intervals, no matter how often she pushed the button. She knew that, but it gave her an element of control over the pain.

Once in the night, the machine awakened her with beeping. A nurse bustled into her vision, changed the morphine bag, took her vital signs and left after a few soothing words.

After an interminable time of waking and sleeping, she heard Jo's voice. "Open your eyes, sweetheart. Time to eat breakfast."

Struggling up out of a drugged tunnel, she saw daylight.

Jo was squeezing her arm. "It's not like you to sleep through a meal."

Seeing the food on the bed table, she wondered when it had come. "I'm not hungry."

"Humor me. Come on, I'll help." Jo offered her a bite of scrambled eggs.

A horrifying glimpse of herself paralyzed, of always having to be fed like a baby, flashed through her mind.

"I don't want to live if I can't move. Do you understand, Jo?"

The fork with the eggs shook. "You're going to be all right."

"Promise me, Jo. They're still asking if I can feel my fingers and toes."

Jo sighed. "I can't, Maggie. I love you too much."

"You'd get over it soon enough if you had to take care of me all the time. You'd hate me. Promise you'll help me die if that happens."

"Then will you eat something?"

"Yes." Jo hadn't promised anything, she knew, but it was too tiring to insist any longer.

At noon Nancy and Liz urged Jo to take a break. They had returned late that morning from the cottage Jo and Maggie had rented. "Let's go to the cafeteria, Jo," Liz suggested.

"All right. I want to phone the office anyway. I'll call the magazine too, Maggie. Neither one of us will be working for a while."

Maggie hadn't even thought about her job, hadn't thought about either one of them taking time off. She'd worked hard coming up through the ranks to her present position as art director at *Leisure Magazine*. And Jo's job as an alcohol and drug abuse counselor was as demanding as her own. Of course, technically they were both still on vacation.

Shortly after Jo and Liz left the room, a woman rapped on the open door and walked up to the bed. "Remember me?" She sounded hesitant, not quite sure of her welcome.

Maggie smiled in recognition. "Yes." Who could forget those brilliantly lit, light blue eyes? She now noticed the blonde hair, the athletic figure. "I'm sorry, I can't remember your name."

"It'd be a miracle if you did," she said. "It's Erica. I'd shake hands, but we already did that." She flashed a white smile.

"Nancy, Erica was the first person to reach me after I took that nose-dive into the pavement."

When Jo returned with Liz, Nancy introduced everyone.

"Do you play softball?" Jo asked, looking confused.

Erica shook her head. "Not anymore." She gestured at the bed. "I see Maggie's being well taken care of."

Jo's lips compressed. "We try."

Nancy said, "Erica saw the accident."

"She held my hand," Maggie added.

"I guess we owe you thanks."

Erica shrugged. "Anyone would have done the same." She grinned at Maggie. "Now I have to keep tabs on you. You know what they say when you rescue someone, that you're responsible for that person. Do you mind if I visit again?"

"I hope you do. I don't even remember the accident, it happened so fast."

"I know. If I'd blinked, I would've missed it."

"I'd like to hear about it sometime, maybe not now," Jo said, looking from Erica to Maggie.

"Sure, whenever." Erica stood nearly a head taller than Jo. "I better go. I'll see you tomorrow then. Maybe I can be of some use."

"That'll be nice," Maggie said.

III

Jo walked Erica to the elevator.

"Tell me," Jo said.

"It was scary. I couldn't believe my eyes. There she was pedaling down this hill, and all of a sudden she was thrown headfirst onto the road." She glanced sideways at Jo. "Sorry. It must be upsetting to hear about it."

"I want to know what happened."

"The bike just flew out from under her. Blood

splattered everywhere. She was on her head, looking out of the tops of her eyes, and then she rolled over. It looked very bad. It seems like she's going to be all right, though."

"She has to be," Jo said before turning back toward the room.

In the parking lot Erica climbed behind the wheel of her Oldsmobile Cutlass and nearly backed into a car pulling out of a space behind her. Heart pounding, she slammed on the brakes and cursed under her breath. It was the third time since yesterday that she had almost collided with another vehicle. Promising herself that she would pay better attention, she drove out into traffic.

She pictured Maggie on the road after the accident, then as she had just seen her. She had walked into Maggie's room, fearing the worst, and been relieved to find her in better shape than she'd thought possible.

She and Dave had returned home last night from a long weekend of camping. Both liked to camp, hike, run. That was why she had believed a relationship with him might work. And she'd thought it had been working, that they got on extremely well.

A horn blasted, brakes squealed, and she realized with dismay that she had run a red light. A hot spurt of fear shot through her, leaving her weak, and she determined to stop mulling things over from behind the wheel. She might kill someone.

Dave owned a condominium. She had moved in with him a little over a year ago, to share expenses and, she thought, to share each other's spare hours. At the time, she had been floundering financially. She wasn't now, though, since she'd become the principal of Stonehurst Elementary School.

"Where you been?" Dave asked, turning as she walked into the kitchen.

"At the hospital, visiting Maggie." She set two grocery bags on the counter.

"I fixed dinner. You hungry?"

She started emptying the bags. "It's only five-thirty, Dave." She was having a hard time sustaining her anger toward him.

"How's she doing?" He moved to put away the groceries.

"She's not paralyzed anyway. She doesn't look much better than she did yesterday, though. They put her in a halo."

"I'd like to go with you tomorrow or join you there."

She looked at him, a slender man with a runner's build. "Well, you'll fit right in."

"What does that mean?"

"Look, Dave, I think I should move out." She had already moved into the spare bedroom.

He was stretching to put dry-goods on the top shelves. "You just bought all these groceries." Turning, he gave her a troubled look. "Just kidding. I'm sorry, Erica. I thought we would work. You're so attractive."

"For a woman."

"Well, yes. Must you qualify it?"

"You do," she shot back, realizing the unfairness of this attack. He had been honest with her last night. "Why did you wait so long to tell me?"

"Let's eat. We'll discuss it over dinner."

Pointing a roll at her, shaking it for emphasis, he talked between bites. "When I saw that bicycle accident, I realized how unexpectedly things change. But for the grace of God or whatever, that might've been me lying on the road. And I knew I would hate myself if I died without ever living honestly." He took another mouthful and she waited impatiently for him to swallow. "I wasn't being fair to you or to me. You know? You deserve someone who can give you a full life." Sipping his wine, he asked, "Anyway, don't you want to know if the man you live with is gay?"

Surprised at how hungry she was in spite of the conversation, she found herself picturing the women in Maggie's room. They were appealing, comfortable to be with.

She recalled Becky, who had caught her pitches in high school and flipped towels with her after showering, who had touched her whenever and wherever possible. She had justified it as the close- ness that comes from playing ball together, until rumors began floating around the school halls that Becky and a cheerleader were caught kissing in the john. She had kept Becky at a distance after that, and felt only a few pangs of remorse when Becky had overdosed on her mother's valium and moved to another school district.

Then there was Lisa, whose position as first base person at Whitewater had made her an ideal roommate. She attributed their frequent and exciting rolls around the bed to hormones and convenience.

Since then, women had come on to her rather

21

often, especially at the Y when she changed or showered. She saw it in their eyes, in how they carried themselves and spoke to her.

Was she herself in full-blown denial, using Dave as he had used her — as a smoke screen?

"I'm sorry. I love you dearly. I don't want you to move out," he was saying.

His hand rested on hers. She stared at it, thinking it looked too delicate to hang on the end of a man's wrist.

She met his unhappy gaze and laughed a little. His eyes looked like they belonged on a labrador. "Just not passionately."

Giving her a wry, grief-stricken smile, he said, "Don't, Erica."

She met Dave in the hospital lobby the next afternoon. He was carrying a Christmas cactus that was blooming in July. He was right, she thought. She didn't want a sexual relationship with him, not if he was gay.

He pushed the elevator button. "Think she'll remember me?"

"I don't know. She remembered me." They stepped onto the carpeted elevator and she pressed five.

"She was holding your hand, looking into your eyes, not mine."

As they turned into Maggie's room, she wondered about their welcome. She'd noticed Jo's reluctant hospitality yesterday. Jo, sitting in a chair by the window, looked at them with the same expression she'd worn yesterday — one of reserved curiosity and surprise.

An old woman, mumbling in her sleep, occupied the bed nearest the door. Her white hair stood on end and one side of her face drooped downward, an apparent stroke victim. She hadn't been there yesterday.

"Maggie, Jo, this is Dave. He was the other runner Monday, the one who called the ambulance." Holding the cactus toward Maggie, he said, "For you. Prickly but pretty. From both of us."

Jo took the plant and set it on the windowsill with others, none of which looked too healthy. Constant sunshine, combined with the air conditioning, quickly withered even the most hardy plants.

"Thanks," Maggie said. "I remember there were two of you." Rods attached the halo to a vest, partially concealed by the hospital gown she wore.

"You look different," Erica said. "Something new has been added to your halo."

"Oh, the vest." Maggie tapped the hard plastic of the exterior. "And the rods."

"The rods bolt the halo to the vest to keep the break in place. It's called mobile traction," Jo explained. "They're going to get her up tomorrow."

"Already?" She couldn't believe any doctor in his right mind would let Maggie out of bed.

"Well, you know, the whole concept of health care has changed. Now doctors and hospitals get patients on their feet as quick as possible." Dave shrugged and looked apologetic as she and Jo stared at him. "I sell pharmaceuticals."

Maybe he spent a lot of time in clinics and

23

hospitals and doctors' offices, but Maggie's case was surely different, Erica thought. It was a broken neck, after all.

Nancy and Liz walked in and she lost her train of thought. They looked like sisters — both a little shorter than her and taller than Jo, with wide shoulders and large breasts, their hair and eyes a light shade of brown. She introduced them to Dave.

"You were the other jogger?" Nancy said with surprise, shaking his hand. "Haven't seen you at Brothers and Sisters in a long time."

Liz also knew him, giving him a hug as if he were a long lost friend.

Erica felt herself blush. Brothers and Sisters was the gay bar in town. She was filled with fear, then anger. He flinched when she met his soft brown eyes.

She was shunted to the side, near the old woman's bed. Startled, she noticed that the old lady was now awake and looking at her out of rheumy, pale blue eyes, reaching for her with a claw-like hand.

She caught Jo's attention across Maggie's bed. "What's her name? Maggie's roommate."

"Mrs. Stepanski," Jo replied over the babble of voices.

Involuntarily, she took Mrs. Stepanski's hand. The skin felt paper-thin and loose, the veins thick. She smiled. "Hello." And as the trays were carried in, "Dinner's here."

A nurse followed the tray-carrier. The din of conversation died. There were too many people in the room. Perhaps some of them would be expelled. Instead the nurse said, "Please don't enable either of these patients by feeding them."

Erica frowned. She sat down next to Mrs. Stepanski's bed and watched the old lady's struggle to feed herself. Her head and arm and hand shook. When she finally got the fork to her mouth and found the food had fallen off, her eyes filled with tears.

Fuck this enabling shit, she thought angrily and said gently, "Let me."

"Th . . . th . . . th . . ."

"The pleasure is mine." She scooped the soup off Mrs. Stepanski's chin and into her mouth. Behind her she heard laughter and teasing as Maggie tried to feed herself, apparently throwing her dinner over her shoulder. When she couldn't bend her head, how could she see either the fork or her plate to coordinate hand to mouth?

When she and Dave left Maggie's room, they met a short, handsome woman coming in. With her were two young people, a girl in her late teens and a boy in mid-adolescence. The girl was tall and slender with shoulder-length dark hair and blue-gray eyes, Maggie's eyes. The boy was also tall and so skinny that his wrist bones looked disproportionately large. He had thick, light brown hair and tawny eyes, shaded by long, fair lashes. She did a double-take.

"Think those are her kids? The girl looks like Maggie," she said to Dave as they hurried toward the elevator.

"And maybe her sister," he added.

They had driven her Cutlass. It was more comfortable than Dave's four-wheel-drive F-150 pickup. The sky glowed with diffused light. Reluctant to go home, unwilling to be inside, she drove around Riverside Park, past the huge lake and the river feeding it. A warm breeze, creating the waves on which ducks bobbed, brought the smells of water and fish and weeds through the car's open windows.

It occurred to her that one of the things she liked so much about Dave was her own comfort level with him. He never appeared threatened when she was assertive. When she changed the oil in his truck, he thanked her and fixed dinner. His behavior was so different from the other men in her life.

"Don't move out, Erica." He brushed his thinning curls out of his face. "Who's going to rotate my tires?"

She laughed. "Who's going to cook for me if I leave?" She shot him a glance, thinking that men with curly hair were more likely to go bald than those with no natural curl. Instead of head hair, they seemed to grow masses of body hair. His curled out of his shirt-front. She recalled the feel of his body, bony against her own. "Not yet I won't." But she couldn't resist saying, "You should have told me."

"It's a hard thing to admit to your girlfriend. I thought you might be the solution to my sexuality. You're attractive — physically, mentally."

What was it that drew one male to another, she wondered. Two hard, hairy bodies moving in unison. You'd think they'd welcome the softness of a woman — the gentle curves, the smooth skin. Although her college roommate had been as lean and athletic as she herself was, her skin had been silky, her breasts and buttocks miniature mounds of malleable flesh.

"You guessed right, they're lesbians," Dave said.

"Really? I wasn't sure." Guilt by association. She

26

noticed that her heart was pounding. She felt the hot flush on her cheeks.

"Sweetie, they're nice people. Supportive."

She had to admit she longed to know them better, wanted to understand their relationships, to share their interests, to gain their acceptance.

IV

Maggie eyed the physical therapist warily as he made his way around the end of the bed. She had been dreading his arrival.

"My name's Tony. I'm the guy who's going to take you for a walk." A slight man, dressed in green scrubs, he smiled down at her. "We'll just go to the end of the hall and back."

"Do I have to?" The pain lay curled in a ball at the base of her skull. She knew better than to disturb it. The nurse had tried to wash the blood out of her hair yesterday before she had been fitted with the vest. Her skin, even her hair hurt. If someone had told her that hair could hurt before all of this, she would have laughed.

"If you want to go home, we have to get you on your feet. Doctor's orders."

With help she struggled to a sitting position, let her legs slide off the bed and stood up. Expecting to be weak, she staggered instead under the crushing weight of the halo. Horrified, she sat down again.

"Dizzy?" he asked, fastening a belt around her robe.

"Yes," she lied, thinking maybe he wouldn't make her walk if he thought she might pass out.

"Let's just go a short way." He helped her to her feet again.

She looked at Jo, saw the helplessness in her face. "I can't. It feels like there's a ton of bricks on my head. Something's wrong."

"Sure, you can," he said.

Given no choice, she did what she had done the day of the accident. She put the pain on the back burner. Hunched forward with arms akimbo, she carried the halo with her shoulders. Hearing Jo's sharp intake of breath as she shuffled toward the door, she was suddenly angry at her inability to stop this charade. There was nothing to do but grit her teeth and get through it.

Attached to the physical therapist by his belt, Maggie made her determined way down the hall. She saw the windows at the end, actually only a few doors down. Licking her lips, she concentrated on the blue sky beyond. A boy was standing, framed by the glass, watching her. She must look like a character out of a horror movie, she thought. Frowning, she shuffled to the windows overlooking the river. Looking out, she noticed someone moving about on a moored yacht, resembling a toy on a toy.

"Can we go back now?" she asked through clenched teeth, ignoring the boy who continued to stare.

Turning slowly, she fixed her gaze on Jo and Nancy and Liz. They marked the distance to her door, which looked impossibly far away. When she reached it, she attempted a smile.

Jo helped her back into bed, then left the room.

Maggie lay very still, waiting for the pain to curl back to bearable proportions. They had taken her morphine machine away that morning. Now she had to rely on pills brought every few hours by the nurse. She had sent Jo to ask for one before Tony made his appearance. Perhaps it hadn't had time to take effect.

She was tired. The walk was over, the bed almost comfortable. Jo had arranged the pillows to take some of the weight off the screws in the back of her head. Sleep edged up on her, and she gratefully gave herself to it.

Erica shifted the vase of roses she had cut from the bushes outside the patio door. She stood in front of the bank of elevators with Maggie's relatives — Katherine, presumably the sister, and the kids, Shelley and Mike. Searching for something to say, she finally asked, "How long will you be staying in town?" The elevator doors opened.

Katherine and Shelley glanced at her. Maggie's daughter looked thin and tense. Katherine's eyes were streaked with red lines. Mike, slouching in a corner of the elevator, was pale.

Katherine said, "I don't know. Nice roses. Maggie loves flowers."

"Thanks." Perhaps such a serious accident precluded normal conversation. It seemed inappropriate to ask questions. What did Katherine do? Was Mike involved in sports? Did Shelley work or go to school? When the doors slid open on the fifth level, they walked in silence toward Maggie's room.

She edged past Mrs. Stepanski as the old lady stuttered some unintelligible reply to her greeting. Starting toward the window ledge, crowded with Maggie's plants, she stopped and with a smile put the home-grown roses on the table next to the old woman's bed. "For you," she said, glancing at Maggie who appeared to be sleeping. Tomorrow she would bring another floral offering.

"Nice touch," Katherine said.

As Mrs. Stepanski struggled with thanks, she squeezed her hand. "You're welcome."

She caught Jo's eyes on her, noticed the slight smile and nod, and her heart swelled a little. A new person sat next to the bed, facing Jo and Maggie.

Maggie was listening to the conversation taking place over her as she feigned sleep. That was one of the perks of being hurt. She didn't have to talk to anyone she didn't want to. She heard Jo's eager questions about the softball team. Had Gail been playing tennis? Golf?

"Maggie can't seem to stay awake," Jo said. "Want to take a walk?"

"Sure." Maggie heard Gail's chair squeak when she stood up.

"Have you met Katherine and the kids?" Jo asked.

"Yes, we've met. It's good to see you again," Gail said. "Sorry about the circumstances."

Jo introduced her to Erica then.

"Haven't I seen you someplace before? Do you play softball?" Gail asked.

Erica said, "I did. Played in high school. Even managed to get a softball scholarship to college."

"Really? Where'd you go?"

"Whitewater."

"I played shortstop and first base for Point. Maybe we competed against each other."

"Perhaps. Fifteen, sixteen years ago."

"Yeah. That'd be about right," Gail replied.

"Excuse us for a minute," Jo said. "We'll be right back."

Maggie opened her eyes, and Erica walked over. "How's it going?"

"All right, I guess. Have you met my family?"

Smiling at Kat and the kids, Erica said, "Unofficially."

When Jo and Gail returned, Erica was spooning food into Mrs. Stepanski's mouth. She acknowledged them with a glance.

Gail paused. "Anything good for dinner?"

"Creamed chicken, mixed veggies, applesauce. Looks okay."

"Are you hungry?"

Erica cleared her throat nervously. "Getting there. I have to go home soon, though."

"Where's home?" Gail laughed a little. "If that's too nosy, don't answer. I'm always sticking my foot in my mouth."

"I live here in town." She glanced at Gail, thinking she looked like an athlete. She was tanned and slender, as if she spent hours in the sun exercising.

Maggie's world narrowed when visitors left, as the hospital lights dimmed and voices became murmurs. She hated the length of the nights, the quiet that failed to distract her, the shadowy corner of the room that disoriented her. Hearing Mrs. Stepanski's garbled speech, noticing her call light flashing, she buzzed the nurse.

Earlier in the evening, Mrs. Stepanski had had visitors for the first time — four people who sat around her bed and talked among themselves, then left after less than an hour.

When a young woman swished into the room on silent feet, Maggie jerked a thumb at the other bed. "She needs help."

She bristled when the nurse, young enough to be Mrs. Stepanski's granddaughter, admonished the old lady. "Ethel, you have to stop calling for us all the time. We can't spend the entire night in here."

"I ky yi yi beshan."

With only a little fumbling, Maggie slipped a

book-on-tape into the boombox that Jo had brought from home. She was becoming adept at doing things by touch.

"I'll put you on the bedpan." The nurse briskly drew the curtain, shutting her out but not Mrs. Stepanski's unintelligible words.

She rewound the tape and pushed play, then fell asleep almost immediately at the soothing sound of the reader's voice. When she woke again, the curtain was still drawn around Mrs. Stepanski's bed. She heard moaning, saw the flashing light. Surely the old woman wasn't still on the bedpan? She pushed her button and an older nurse showed up. Had they changed shifts?

She gestured. "Help her, please."

Before the nurse left the room, she took her vital signs and gave her a pain pill.

When her room was suddenly filled with people talking and moving behind Mrs. Stepanski's curtain, she thought she must be dreaming. She tried to open her eyes, to pull herself into consciousness, to find out what was going on. Her throat felt parched, and she managed to close her mouth. When she awoke once more, an empty bed was being wheeled into the room.

She realized then that Mrs. Stepanski had died. She hoped the woman hadn't spent her last moments alone, on the bedpan, her light flashing. Had anyone cared? Those friends and relatives who came for one short visit? The nurses who refused to answer her summons? Sniffing, she wondered if the elderly woman had known she was a nuisance to everyone.

She sobbed herself back to sleep.

V

Around nine p.m. on Friday, when everybody was readying to leave, Dr. Hartland marched into Maggie's room, a nurse on his heels. "Come on, little woman. We're going for a Friday night stroll," he said to Maggie.

"It's late," Jo protested. "Can't it wait till tomorrow?"

"Nope," Hartland said. "We've got a date here."

The nurse helped Maggie to her feet, while the others watched.

In the hallway, Hartland walked backwards,

taunting Maggie, "Care to dance? You can walk faster than that. You want to go home, don't you?"

The nurse, holding Maggie's arm, said, "Be brave. It can't hurt that much."

She tasted anger. Who was this woman anyway? "How do you know what it feels like? Did you ever break your neck?"

"No, but . . ."

"Well, don't tell me how it hurts then."

They reached the stairs. Hartland pushed open one of the doors. "Let's see you go up and down the steps."

She hated him. "I don't have to go up and down stairs at home." But she climbed them anyway, the doctor behind her, the nurse next to her. She wouldn't show them any weakness.

"Good, good. Tomorrow we can talk about dismissing you. Let's go back to your room."

She wanted to leave tonight, now. The knot of friends and relatives parted to let her through. She could see their anger.

"Atmosphere's a little frigid in here," Hartland remarked as the nurse helped Maggie settle back in bed. "Maybe Sunday you can pack your bag," he said to her.

"Do we need to get anything special for her care?" Jo asked, her voice icy.

"A riser for the toilet," Hartland said, barely giving her a glance. "And the hardware to adjust the halo. She'll need that with her at all times, in case there's a change in the traction. If there is, call me. If I'm not available, take her to the nearest medical facility. Otherwise, let her do what she thinks she can do." He turned on his heel and they made way for him. "See you tomorrow."

"How will we know if something's wrong?" Maggie murmured. "It feels like it's not right now."

Jo took her hand. "Don't cry."

"I want out of here. I'll do anything, walk anywhere, but I'm gone from here by Sunday." As if the pain wasn't enough . . . "If Bill were here, Hartland wouldn't dare treat me like he did." Perhaps the neurosurgeon had contempt for them. He must know they were lesbians.

Jo attempted to comfort Maggie, but the more she tried, the harder Maggie cried. And then, as if he had been notified, Bill called.

"Yes, I'm crying," Maggie admitted. She sniffed and drew a deep breath that ended in a sob. "If I were a man, if you were here, Hartland wouldn't dare do what he did tonight."

"He must have had a reason," Bill remarked after hearing what she had to say, and she wondered why his voice still had the power to soothe her.

Did terrible things happen for a reason? "Maybe I'm being punished," she muttered. He didn't reply at first, and she watched Jo leave the room. Before breaking her neck, she would never have said such a thing in front of Jo or to Bill. She wouldn't have admitted any doubts, nor would she have risked Jo's hurt anger.

"For what?" he finally said.

"I don't know. It just shouldn't have happened."

"It was a freak accident, all right. I talked to Shelley last night. She said you're a real tough lady."

When she hung up, Jo returned.

"Some doctor. I ought to beat the shit out of him," Mike said suddenly, and the others stared at him. He spoke so seldom.

Liz cleared her throat. "Maggie's resisted getting up. Maybe he was making her mad enough to want to get out of here."

Erica had gone to the hospital yesterday, Sunday afternoon, to discover that Maggie had been dismissed that morning. She hadn't expected her to be released so soon — only six days after the accident. Saturday there had been an emergency at school, a broken water main. Why they had called her in, she didn't know, except that the office had been flooded. She had stayed and worked late, studying next year's curriculum, and never gotten to the hospital.

Dave called her from work Monday. "You have their address, their phone number. Why don't you call or go over there? They don't bite."

If he was trying to make her feel better, he wasn't succeeding. "Why don't you go with me?"

"I'm going to the grocery store after work. I'll have something for you to eat when you get home."

"You don't have to cook for me."

"Consider it a bribe. I want you to take my truck in for a tune-up before you go back to work regularly."

"I'll take it in if you go with me to see Maggie this first time."

"Okay. You got me by the short hairs. I'll take off around four and swing by to pick you up."

They parked out front. Nancy, who was cutting

the lawn, let the mower die. Fresh cut grass speckled her bare legs. "Hey, we wondered where you disappeared to over the weekend. Good to see you." She shook Dave's hand, gave Erica a hug.

Warmed by the embrace, she forgot her fear of a weak welcome. Nancy walked inside with them. Sunshine splashed through the many open windows, warming the rooms and floors. She looked around, thinking she would never feel trapped indoors in this house.

"Guess who's here," Nancy called as they entered the living room.

Maggie smiled as they walked around the chair to stand in her line of vision. "I missed you."

"Hi." Jo joined them, coming out of the hall. "Sit. Can I get you something to drink? Anything?"

"A Coke or a Pepsi would be great," Dave said. "Diet if you have it."

"You know, I won't be going back to work until August," Erica offered. "I can mow the yard, run errands, clean house."

"Thanks. We gratefully accept all offers."

Dave said, "Well, I do meals on wheels. In fact, I have bags of food in the car."

"And he's a marvelous chef," Erica put in, giving him a grateful glance.

Humming a tuneless rendition of "Summertime," Dave checked out the kitchen. His suggestion that he fix enchiladas, Spanish rice and refried beans for supper had met with an enthusiastic response. "Want to help?" he asked Erica.

She figured she owed him and willingly chopped onions and grated cheese, while watching birds flit through the back yard. Rushing into the living room when she spied a pair of Baltimore orioles, she said, "They're almost gaudy, aren't they?" But so was the more common cardinal. It was the seldom seen who were most appreciated, she thought.

"You like birds?" Maggie's chair was aimed at the bay window to give her the best view.

"My mother had feeders all over the yard. I grew up not far from here, on Cherry Street."

"Does she still live there?"

"No. My dad died and she moved to Arizona." She missed her mother, visited her often.

"You deserted your post," Dave called.

Maggie ate little. Opening her mouth and chewing clearly took more determination and energy than she apparently possessed right now.

"Let me cut your food for you," Jo said, offering her a few mouthfuls.

"It's good but I'm full," Maggie replied, returning to her chair and falling asleep, just as she had slept through their conversations in the hospital.

Maggie sat by the window and watched Thursday unfold. The night lifted, revealing a blue sky dotted with puffs of clouds. She observed the march of sun across the southern sky. A soft breeze filtered the smells of cut grass and roses through the screens. The pair of orioles pecked at orange halves hanging from the bird feeders; and cardinals, goldfinches, purple finches, doves, nuthatches and chickadees flew from the trees to the feeders and back again — a flying food line.

She wondered if she would always feel so fragile,

as if she might shatter at any untoward bump. She had been unable to find a comfortable sleeping position in the double bed and now sat up even when sleeping.

Katherine had left for Milwaukee Monday morning, taking Shelley and Mike with her. She loved her kids, was always glad to see them, but was relieved when they left. She couldn't stop behaving like a mother in their presence — hiding her pain, her worries, taking on their concerns. And she had no strength for pretense or anyone else's agenda.

Liz and Nancy checked in every day, often helping Jo with her care or doing necessary chores around the house and yard. Erica had been over every day since the enchilada dinner Monday night, and Dave had brought last night's meal on wheels.

Nancy and Jo had washed her hair earlier in the week, wrapping her in plastic garbage bags to protect the vest, seating her on a plastic lawn chair in the tub. She had quickly become exhausted. The next day Liz had found some dry shampoo and Nancy and Jo had used it on her today. Her hair was dark again, laced sparsely with strands of gray. She had turned forty-five a month before the accident, a week after Jo had celebrated her thirty-fifth birthday.

Jo brought the Betadine ointment and dressed the wounded flesh around the screws, something she did every day. Then she put Polysporin on the stitches in Maggie's forehead. "How you doing, hon?"

"Okay. Want to go for a walk? You must be tired of being cooped up."

"I can go out any time, but if you feel like walking, we'll do it."

Actually, Maggie didn't want to do anything that

41

might unleash the pain, but she longed to get better, to retrieve some strength, to do more than sit and sleep. Hadn't they made her walk at the hospital as if walking was the key to renewed health? She stood up and slipped a hand under Jo's arm. "Now it's okay for me to hold your arm or hand. We should take advantage of this, darling. Disability has its perks."

The pain shifted when she stepped off the stoop. Wincing at the new pressure, she paused momentarily to look inward, hoping she'd been mistaken. But something had changed. Not more than fifty feet from the door, she stopped altogether. "I can't, Jo. Let's go back." They had crept that far. Now they turned. The front door looked unattainably far. It brought to mind her first walk at the hospital with Tony.

"What is it?"

"I don't know. It hurts something fierce."

Jo said no more until they were back in the house. "Are you better now?" She watched Maggie intently as she lowered herself into the armchair.

Maggie shut her eyes. "No." The pain, always present before, had become a fearful thing.

"I'll call Hartland's office." Jo started for the phone.

Maggie recalled her walk with Hartland Friday night at the hospital. "No. I'm going to see him Monday. I'll wait."

Sitting at the table that evening, Maggie dropped her piece of pizza onto her plate. If opening her mouth had been a chore before and chewing difficult, they were now almost impossible. Tears rolled silently down her face. She did nothing to stop them. The pain had become a monster, pounding at the base of her skull.

Jo, Nancy and Liz froze momentarily in their chairs. Nancy, who was closest to Maggie, touched her arm. Jo leaped to her feet.

"Sit down, Jo," Maggie ordered. She'd make it to Monday. She wouldn't let Hartland think she was a sissy. Thank God her kids couldn't see her like this.

That night she got up from her sleep-sitting position next to Jo and started toward the bathroom. An electric shock of pain shot down her right buttock and leg and nearly drove her to her knees.

On her feet at Maggie's first cry, Jo asked, "What's wrong?" She put her arms around Maggie to hold her up, helped her limp to the bathroom. "Maybe it's from sitting up all the time."

"I can't lie down, I can't sit up. What am I supposed to do?" She felt betrayed by this new, unexpected pain.

VI

Leaving Jo in the anteroom Monday morning, Maggie followed the X-ray technician. First X-rays, then the doctor. That was the pattern. After posing for four exposures, she sat in a chair, waiting. She had learned to wait.

The technician, a buxom woman in a white pantsuit, bustled past her and down the hall. "Stay there. Don't move," she ordered.

She turned her body, saw Hartland striding toward her with the technician. Her heart picked up momentum.

Hartland studied the X-rays for a few moments, then looked at her. "Who brought you here?"

"Jo." She gestured toward the waiting room and noticed his nod at the technician.

"Did you feel something different? Did something happen?" he asked.

"I just stepped off the front step Thursday, that was all," she said. "I didn't want to bother you over the weekend." Friday night's betrayal at the hospital was forgotten, lost in her apprehension, her need of him.

"Next time you let me know if you think something's wrong, no matter when or where or what." Jo joined them, concern on her face, and he turned to her. "Take her to the hospital. The break is out of line." He demonstrated by touching the back of one index fingernail to the opposing fingertip pad. "We need to get it back into position." He aligned the fingertips. "Be very careful. I'll meet you there."

His cautioning words and obvious alarm frightened them into silence. Leaning forward, Maggie wordlessly urged Jo to hurry even though the smallest bumps jarred the pain at the base of her skull. And Jo watched the rearview mirror, fearful, she said, that someone would run into them.

At the hospital Hartland took X-ray after X-ray, against which he checked the slow straightening of Maggie's neck, using the hardware she carried to crank the broken second vertebra back together. Stretching her neck until the ligaments were taut, he backed off the tension until she could once more swallow.

She couldn't help but notice that her head and neck were in a more forward position than before, her chin jutting. And she didn't understand how the new angle could be so different from the last one yet her fracture be pieced together.

Hartland pushed her in a wheelchair to where Jo was waiting. He squeezed Maggie's shoulder, a comforting gesture, then pulled a prescription pad out of the breast pocket of the white jacket covering his suit and began writing and talking. "I want you to rent an electric recliner and a hospital bed. If you have access to a wheelchair, that would be good too. Maggie's insurance should cover any rentals if they're prescribed." He tore a sheet off the pad and handed it to Jo. "You take it easy, Maggie. Call me if anything feels wrong — any time, any day."

Jo watched him disappear around a corner. "Well, that was a switch, wasn't it? I asked him what we needed before you left the hospital, and he just said a riser. Remember?"

"Jo, do you think maybe the vertebra wasn't broken all the way through, and that it is now? Because we weren't careful enough?" Maggie looked into Jo's eyes, saw the reflection of her own fear.

"I don't know, Maggie. We'll never find that out now." Jo shook her head.

When Maggie pushed the right buttons, the electric recliner effortlessly lifted her to her feet, laid her back into a bearable resting position, or sat her up straight so that she could see what was in front of her. She tried the hospital bed, found it uncomfortable, and returned to the recliner. It would become her bed. The cloth donut Jo had bought for her to sit on relieved the pressure on her lower back.

The next day, Tuesday, she was watching Nancy fill the feeders. Nancy taught business classes at one of the area high schools and had summers off. Liz worked at Kimberly Clark in the lab, trying to develop a truly disposable diaper, one that didn't clog the landfills for years. Maggie was grateful that Jo's co-workers were so cooperative, willingly covering for her while she took an extended leave of absence.

She hadn't thought about work since the accident. Len Brewster, her boss, had sent flowers, visited her at the hospital and told her during frequent phone calls not to worry. He'd asked her assistant art director at the magazine to fill in until she recovered.

"How you doing?" Erica asked, walking into her line of vision.

"Better."

"Did you go to your appointment?" Erica sat on the davenport, directly in front of her.

"We ended up at the hospital with Hartland realigning my neck. He prescribed this chair." She demonstrated the chair's capabilities, pushing the lift control. Then, at its apex, she accidentally pressed the down button. The seat dropped a few inches, taking her with it. She felt the break shift again. The discomfort, the new pressure, the increased pain gave it away. "Maybe you better get Jo, Erica."

The days took on their own quality for Maggie. She needed peace but felt more secure with people around her. Summer floated inside through the open windows and patio door, bringing the smells of flowers and junipers and fresh-cut grass, the sounds of lawnmowers growling and children playing and cars motoring by. Those who were with her moved about and talked quietly. Their occasional laughter sometimes caused her to jump, always to smile.

By Friday she knew the broken vertebra had changed position once more, although she couldn't recall doing anything to jostle it. She supposed it could be happening an infinitesimal amount at a time, whenever she moved.

Hartland met them in the waiting room, as usual, and after many X-rays and much wrenching, she was again released. She had an appointment in his office Monday.

On the drive home, she sank into gloom. "I could be in this halo forever, with Hartland cranking my neck back where it belongs every few days." More than two weeks and there had been no healing, she now realized. Hartland had warned her it could happen again, and she felt that her very life depended on him. She had to trust him. The thought of spending months in the halo depressed the hell out of her.

Wordlessly, Jo took her hand in a gesture meant to comfort.

"I've never felt so fucking helpless in my life," she said.

Next Monday morning Maggie and Jo sat in Hartland's office in stunned silence. The neurosurgeon had just told them that on the following Monday he was leaving the country for three weeks. Stating that the break was very unstable, he slid the business card of an orthopedic surgeon across the desk.

Maggie's throat ached. She was unwilling to believe that he would leave her like this. She swallowed tears and heard her voice quaver. "There hasn't been any healing, has there?"

He shook his dark head in agreement. "How can there be when it keeps moving?"

"Do we call this doctor if it moves again?" Jo asked, throwing Maggie a worried look. She was trying to hide her own fear, Maggie saw.

"Go to the hospital. The radiologist can read the X-rays."

"Who will straighten it?" Jo inquired.

"I've already talked to the orthopedic surgeon. He's familiar with your case, and he's very capable. I'm the only neurosurgeon on staff."

"And you're going away," Maggie said bleakly.

He stood up, dismissing them.

In Jo's van, Maggie said dully, "I'm going to die, or worse, be paralyzed."

"You're not going to do either. I won't let it happen. I love you too much," Jo countered fiercely.

"A fucking lot of good that will do." And then, in spite of her efforts not to, she started crying.

"Don't," Jo whispered, crying herself. "I can't see to drive."

"Maybe if I don't move, it won't move either." Perhaps that was the only way, because she knew her chances for recovery without Hartland ranged from remote to nil.

* * * * *

The next morning, she begged Jo, "Let's not go." They had an appointment that day with the vascular surgeon who had stitched her wound.

"We're going, sweetie. I'll drive two miles an hour if I have to."

After removing the stitches, the surgeon marveled over how her forehead had mended. "It's amazing how the body heals itself," he remarked. "I thought Maggie might have to go through plastic surgery."

She snorted. "It doesn't do any good to have an unscarred forehead if you don't have a neck to hold it up."

"You will soon," the doctor assured her. "Are you ready for the fusion?"

She gave him a blank, startled look. "What fusion?"

He pursed his lips and glanced from one woman to the other, then hedged, "Call Dr. Hartland's office. You should hear it from him."

Hartland told her and then Jo on the phone that arrangements had already been made — without consulting either one. There had been no time. Tomorrow morning at ten she would be put on the Theda Star helicopter and flown to Froedtert Hospital in Milwaukee. Her second and third vertebrae would be fused together Thursday morning by a team of surgeons, headed by a highly qualified neurosurgeon. "Dr. Spencer, one of the best." They were only waiting for permission from Maggie's insurance company, he said.

Again shocked into silence, they sat motionless at the table for several minutes. Finally, Jo covered

50

Maggie's hand with her own and put enthusiasm into her voice. "Once it's fused, it won't move anymore."

"I won't be able to turn my head, will I?" Was that so awful, though, when weighed against being alive and mobile?

Jo met her troubled gaze. "I don't know, Maggie. That's not what I meant. You need to call your kids and Kat. If you want, I'll call our friends."

Maggie spent the night in the recliner, wrapped in a blanket. Alternating between relief and anxiety, she remembered all the horror stories she had heard about surgery — healthy organs being removed, too much anesthesia administered resulting in death or coma, surgical instruments and wads of cotton left behind in the body, AIDS contracted through blood transfusions, blood clots that stopped the heart. Suppose they rendered her quadriplegic through bungling?

When the Halcyon put her to sleep, she dreamed that the surgeons transferred her neck to someone else.

VII

The helicopter beat its way skyward, while Maggie's pulse kept time with the rotors. It was more like being on a carnival ride than an aircraft. Afraid of heights, she watched with alarm as Erica and Liz, heads thrown back, mouths agape, became unidentifiable with distance.

The nurse taking her blood pressure said, "What is it?"

"I'm a little scared." Her view was restricted to the lower edge of the small, circular window next to her. When they had wanted to strap her to a board for the trip, she had pleaded to be allowed to sit up. She knew she couldn't spend forty-five minutes pinned down with the halo on.

The noise of the rotors held conversation to a minimum. There were four of them in the tiny interior — herself, two nurses and the pilot. Staring through the bit of window, she saw a toy-size landscape complete with miniature buildings and figures. Tearing herself away from the view, she looked instead into the nurse's sky-blue eyes and refused to think about how high up she was and what would happen if she fell.

By the time the helicopter set down on a patch of pavement outside the hospital complex, she had returned her focus inward. She was still getting through the days one minute at a time.

The emergency section for the medical complex was located in Milwaukee General. It consisted of several smaller rooms wrapped around a large space. She was wheeled by the helicopter attendant to one of these rooms, where she waited.

Through the open door, she watched and listened to the drama surrounding her. A man rocked soundlessly, his face in his hands. A screaming child sat on the lap of a young woman, who held the little boy in a tight embrace. A huge black man with a bloody leg wound was carried on a gurney to her room, placed on the other bed and the curtain drawn around him. She heard his moans and curses, the nurses and doctor and accompanying policeman talking to him and to one another. She registered these happenings to share with Jo.

Jo found her toward the end of that first hour, and they greeted each other with smiles and a sense of relief. Neither wanted to be without the other in this unfamiliar setting.

Waiting for Gail to arrive Thursday morning, Erica watched for her through the living room window while Dave finished getting ready for work.

"Give my best to everyone. Tell Maggie it's about time she got her head on straight," he said, knotting his tie in front of the hall mirror. He met her eyes in the reflection. "Just kidding. I'll be waiting to hear how it goes."

Erica tried to reassess her emotions. She had succumbed to an urgent need to go to Milwaukee, to be there when Maggie emerged from surgery. Gail had called and offered her a ride. Although why Gail was going she didn't know since she'd only seen her once at the hospital.

"I'll call when it's over," she promised. It had been wrenching, frightening, to see Maggie carried off in the helicopter. She felt a touch of fear. All any of them could do now was hope that the surgery went well.

"I don't remember a Gail."

"You didn't meet her. I haven't seen much of her."

"Liz isn't going down for the operation?"

"She's going Friday after work. Then she'll stay the weekend with Nancy and Jo."

A silver Ford Probe parked out front, and Gail got out and walked toward the condo.

Erica said goodbye, grabbed her book bag and purse and went outside. "I'm all set."

"So this is where you live."

Lowering herself into the sporty car, she looked toward the condo and saw Dave come out the door. He waved at her and locked the door behind him. She felt a need to explain him and squelched it.

"You have a roommate," Gail said.

"Yes. He owns the place."

They drove in silence until they reached Highway 41, where they stopped for coffee at the Citgo station. As they took the ramp onto the highway, she asked Gail how well she knew Maggie and Jo.

Gail smiled tightly and stared straight ahead. "I know Jo a whole hell of a lot better than Maggie. We were lovers for years."

Startled, she stammered, "I didn't know."

"We bought the house she lives in together."

She frowned and swallowed some coffee. The hot liquid spurted up her nose, burning the delicate membranes.

"You all right?" Gail asked, patting her on the back.

Struggling to draw a deep breath, she nodded. "It went down the wrong pipe, I guess." She fumbled in her purse for a tissue and blew her nose.

"Revelations 101," Gail murmured.

"Where do you live now?"

"In an apartment." Gail shot her a look. "You didn't know that Jo and I were once a couple?"

"I don't know much of anything about anybody in this group."

"Well, our parting was not good. I met someone. Jo bought out my half of the house."

"I see." Just like a divorce. "When did she and Maggie . . ."

"They met three years ago, shortly after Maggie moved here from Milwaukee. They started living together a little over a year ago. My romance fell apart when my new lover accepted a job-transfer to Chicago. I didn't want to move out of the area, so our affair died with distance." Gail shrugged and gave her an ironic smile. "All for naught. Are you and your roommate involved?"

"What?" She had been thinking about the all-for-naught comment. Was that what her relationships boiled down to? "We used to be. Not anymore."

Gail snorted. "The grass always looks greener on the other side, doesn't it? Hindsight is twenty-twenty. Overused clichés, but still applicable."

"You think you should have stayed with Jo, you mean?"

Gail shrugged. "I don't know. I wasn't satisfied at the time or I wouldn't have done what I did. I don't have any answers." She ran long fingers through her dark hair, momentarily straightening the curls. "How do you manage to stay with this guy now that you're uninvolved?"

"His name is Dave, and he's gay."

They arrived at Froedtert jittery from drinking coffee and desperate to find a bathroom. Directed to the surgery waiting room, Erica spotted Jo and Nancy immediately and then noticed Kat and Maggie's children. She crossed the room followed by Gail and found herself engulfed in a hug by Jo, then Nancy.

"It'll be a long wait," Jo remarked, her eyes on Gail. "The operation takes around four or five hours, and they supposedly started at seven."

At noon the woman at the desk announced that

Maggie was out of surgery and being taken to recovery.

Dr. Spencer, still in scrubs and cap with mask dangling, made an appearance. The white-haired neurosurgeon headed the team of operating surgeons. He said that the fusion had gone well, that several inches of bone had been removed from Maggie's hip and used to fuse the fractured vertebra, C-2, to the next vertebra, C-3. She should be out of recovery and in ICU within an hour or two.

The hours passed slowly. At three in the afternoon they still had no further word on Maggie's condition. Another woman had replaced the earlier attendant at the desk. She shook her head when asked. "I just called down. She's still in recovery."

Erica stood on the periphery looking in. At least that's how she perceived herself. Only Gail had less reason to be there. She watched Jo shuffle through magazines, then put them down and pace. Maggie's kids did the same. Katherine read. Liz and Gail talked quietly among themselves and to the others. And she couldn't hold a thought. She'd brought a novel along, but she read the same paragraph over and over until the print ran together. She went for short walks, but as soon as she left the waiting room, she wanted to rush back. Her body was stretched taut, her nerves irritatingly sensitive. She wanted to scream, to run, and instead had to force herself into a false patience.

At five only those waiting for word on Maggie were left in the room. When the phone rang, Erica jumped. She held her breath as the attendant picked up the receiver, studying the woman for some body language that would indicate the long wait was over, that Maggie had emerged from surgery and recovery as well as possible. The woman smiled. Erica exhaled, her muscles suddenly weak.

"You go see her first, Jo," Kat whispered, nudging Jo. "Tell them you're her sister or they might not let you in."

Maggie was in a cubicle separated from others like it by curtains. Somewhere above the head of her bed was a heart monitor, she knew, the lines of life zigzagging across the screen. She was also hooked up to the inevitable IV's — one dispensing electrolytes, the other offering morphine in measured doses.

She saw from the expression Jo tried to hide that she looked awful. One side of her mouth was grossly swollen, making it difficult to smile. The halo was gone. A protective collar engulfed her neck. "Hi, darling," she said, her voice hoarse with dryness. "Where have you been?"

Jo gave her a sickly smile. "That was my question, sweetie. You're the one who kept us waiting all day."

Maggie touched her mouth gingerly. "I woke up with this tube in my throat and I couldn't breathe. Someone ripped it out. I don't remember anything after that. I must look terrible."

Jo said in a voice as rough as Maggie's, "I can only stay five minutes. Then the kids will come and Kat. Nancy and Gail and Erica are upstairs too. You had us worried." She cleared her throat. "You look wonderful."

"Liar," Maggie said.

"Well, you've lost your instrument of torture. No more screws in the head. It certainly improves your appearance."

"I get to feel a mattress for a few days, until they put me in the cast."

The nights and days in ICU were hair-raising. The man in the next cubicle begged loudly to go home and had to be restrained when he pulled out his IV needles. Maggie was awakened from drug-induced sleep by his shouts. The nurses made no effort to be quiet — calling to each other, talking to the patients in loud voices. There were moans and screams, always without warning.

After a few days of this, she began to wonder how anyone was expected to get well in such an environment. Saturday afternoon a room was finally vacated in the spinal cord unit and she was wheeled out of ICU, accompanied by Jo, Nancy, Liz, Erica, Kat, Shelley and Mike. The rigid no-visitors rule except during stipulated hours had been waived for her — perhaps because she and Jo had pleaded to be excepted, maybe because she was expected to attain full recovery.

Erica perched on the register under the window overlooking the hospital's inner courtyard. She had come to Milwaukee again with Liz on Friday night, turning down Liz's offer to stay with friends as she and Nancy and Jo were doing. Instead, she had rented a motel room at the Best Western to share with Gail, who was driving to Milwaukee this afternoon.

She frowned out the window at the outdoor enclosure, which was crisscrossed with sidewalks, landscaped with flowers and trees, arranged conveniently with tables and chairs — offering an oasis of green in the sterile microcosm of hospital life. People walked through it, sometimes stopping to sit a while.

Studying Maggie and Jo, Nancy and Liz, she thought of Gail. They made a microcosm of their own. She told herself she wanted to become a part of this group as a friend.

At seven that evening, she unlocked the motel room door and walked into the dimly lit room. She'd seen Gail's car in the parking lot and asked at the desk if Gail had picked up a room key.

Gail propped herself up on her elbows on one of the double beds. "I fell asleep, I guess. How's Maggie?" She raked fingers through her dark tangle of hair.

"Getting better." She went to the window, as Gail sat on the edge of the bed and stretched. "Mind if I open the drapes?"

"Of course not."

Glancing outside at the parking lot, she saw it was still steamy from a late afternoon shower. The fan hummed, creating an air-conditioned breeze which lifted the hair off her forehead and neck. "Are you hungry? Want to go out to eat?"

"Sounds good. Give me a few minutes to spiff up." Gail disappeared into the bathroom, closing the door behind her.

They drove down the road to a Chinese place, where Erica ordered crabmeat-filled wontons and chicken with broccoli. She sipped Rhine wine and met Gail's gaze across the white tablecloth in the garishly decorated restaurant. Green dragons on red-flocked wallpaper adorned the walls. Brightly colored lanterns hung from a dingy white-tiled ceiling. The black and white checkered floor lent an incongruously practical aspect to the decor. Music piped in over the corner speakers was American pop.

Gail had ordered a Mai Tai and was eating the skewered fruit off the drink. "What do you like to do most?"

She took the inquiry at face value. "Read," she finally answered, the word sounding as if it were a question. Was that true? Did she really prefer reading to hiking, for instance.

Gail looked disappointed. "You don't play racquet-ball or tennis or golf? Or softball anymore?"

"I didn't say that. You asked me what I enjoyed most." She smiled. "I like to be active, too."

Gail grinned. "I'm looking for someone to play tennis and racquetball and occasionally golf with."

"I'd like that." It made her realize that she missed athletics. Dave was not into organized sports.

The waitress set down a plate full of wontons, and she took a bite out of one after dipping it in hot mustard sauce. "These are great. Have some."

The rooms on the spinal cord unit at Froedtert were all singles. When Erica and Gail entered

Maggie's room the next morning, Liz and Nancy and Jo were reading sections of *The Milwaukee Journal.*

Jo looked up. "Well, this is a surprise. Did you meet in the hall or something?"

Gail gave Erica a reassuring smile. "We met last night."

"Where?" she asked.

"At the Best Western."

Erica started to say it wasn't like it sounded, that she and Gail were just friends, but she didn't know how to phrase the explanation so that it wouldn't sound like she was protesting what hadn't been said, only implied.

"Erica?" Maggie called from the bed.

Jo turned back to the newspaper, snapping the pages open.

"How was your night?" Erica asked.

"Long." Maggie looked pale.

"The morphine makes her sick," Jo said.

"Poor Jo. I wouldn't let her leave until late last night. I thought I was going to throw up and choke on it."

VIII

"I'm Tom. I make the casts." He was young and black, and Maggie had seen him in recovery. He was the one who had rushed to her side and jerked the tube out of her mouth. He stood at the foot of her bed. "You're lucky. Since you can't sit up, we're going to put you in a two-piece cast. Be back soon."

When he returned, he removed the Philadelphia collar and flipped her face down on the bed. The backside of the cast was warm, almost hot. He pressed hard, molding it to her head and neck and back, while she struggled for air and frantically pushed the morphine dispensing button. She felt as if her neck might break again.

"I can't breathe," she protested into the mattress.

Jo tried to comfort her, holding her hand, putting cold cloths on the sides of her face, repeatedly saying, "He'll be done soon."

He turned her over. Leaving the room, he came back with the front half of the cast, also warm and pliable, and molded that to her.

She could not look at him. She thought he should have prepared her better, that he might have been more gentle. Feeling invaded, abused, helpless, out-of-control, she wanted to make him feel the same way. And she blamed Jo for letting this happen.

He rolled her onto the molded back of the plastic cast. It covered her from the waist to the top of her head, cupping it, with a band crossing her forehead and holes for her ears. The front half came up under her chin. The two halves were bolted together above her shoulders and belted at the waist. She would be encased in a hard plastic cocoon for the next eight weeks. But at least he hadn't screwed it into her skull, like the halo.

"Don't take it off at all for three weeks," he said. "Then someone can remove the front and wash you, if you lie on your back. Okay?" He looked from her to Jo and then left.

Jo was still wiping tears off Maggie's face. "Shh. I know. He's gone now. It's okay."

Maggie couldn't stop. She didn't even know why she was crying now that he had departed, presumably to torture someone else. She sobbed until the morphine drew her once more down that terrifying and nauseating tunnel into sleep.

That same night, Monday, Dave looked at Erica over the rim of his raised wine glass. "I've met someone."

"Oh? Who?" Her heart thudded against her chest with dismay. She struggled to feel happy for him. "When do I meet him?"

"Wednesday." He held her gaze with his own. "Do you mind if he comes over for dinner?"

"Why would I mind?" But she did. Perhaps she should move, but she didn't want to find another place, to live alone. "Where did you meet him? At the bar?" She looked into his eyes, which were large, brown and doggy-like, and she smiled a little.

"I advertised. You know, gay white male looking for someone with like interests, et cetera. I was afraid I'd get some crazy who was into ball-crunching."

"Tell me about him."

"Well, he's forty, works as a CPA. Bright, nice-looking." He shrugged. "We went out to dinner over the weekend. I like him. I think you will too."

"I'm sure I will." She chewed on her lower lip, her appetite gone.

"It won't change anything here," he promised.

She nodded, feeling like she might cry, knowing, as she was sure he did, that it would change their lives if it went anywhere. "We have to get on with things, both of us."

"Come on, eat," he urged gently, taking a bite of grilled chicken. "It's good."

She smiled a little and forked a piece of white meat. "It always is, Dave." If she left, she'd miss his cooking, his company. "Be careful, will you?"

"I was always careful." He must have seen her worry, her sudden, unspoken indignation. "Erica, I've been tested all along. And I always use condoms."

"Well, make sure that you still do." She'd heard, though, that sometimes the tests weren't accurate. Maybe everyone was running the gauntlet when having sex.

He changed the subject. "Why don't you have Gail over? I'd like to meet her. I'll even cook."

"You better. She might not come back. She's just a friend, you know, Dave." Pushing her plate away, she said, "I'll clean up the kitchen. Then I'm going to bed."

"Hard to go back to work, huh?" He took his dishes to the sink.

When the bedside phone rang, she awoke with a start from a disturbing dream. It vanished into her unconscious even as she grasped for it. Glancing at the clock, seeing how late it was, she feared that something terrible had happened.

"Erica?"

"Is something wrong, Maggie?" Turning on the reading light, she pressed the receiver to her ear. She could barely hear. "You sound so far away."

Maggie spoke louder. "What time is it? I probably woke you up."

"I'm glad. Do you have the cast on?" With a chill she realized she was hearing Maggie cry. "What is it? Where's Jo?"

"She's gone. She needs to get some sleep. It was just a bad day." Maggie told her about the cast-molding.

"Sounds awful."

Maggie's final sob ended in a sigh. "I'll be walking tomorrow. They said I might be able to go home Thursday."

"Hey, that's great. We should have a party." She'd talk to Nancy and Liz about putting up banners.

"It's lonely without you and Nancy and Liz. Jo and I feel deserted." Maggie sounded forlorn.

Erica smiled. "I think of you every day, sometimes several times a day. Don't Katherine and Shelley and Mike live in Milwaukee?"

"Yes." Breaking her neck had brought her kids back, had made Kat contrite. She brightened and nearly laughed for thinking she should have done it sooner. "I'll let you go back to sleep."

"Call me anytime."

"Look. I don't know if Jo would understand my calling at this time of night."

"I won't say anything." Again she felt a chill. She didn't want to alienate Jo.

"Want to go for a walk?" Jo asked. The pain dispenser had been wheeled away, the catheter removed. Maggie was free of encumbrances. "We'll take the wheelchair for when you get tired." Each room had a wheelchair outside its door.

Maggie hadn't been on her feet yet, but surely she wouldn't feel the compression she had experienced in the halo. She put a hand on Jo's back as Jo put slippers on her feet, then helped her into her robe. She was standing, awash with relief. The Minerva cast added weight to her shoulders, held her head and neck immobile, nothing more.

They walked past only two doorways before she asked to sit in the wheelchair. Already she was covered with sweat and trembling with exhaustion, breathing in short gasps. She had at first glanced curiously into doorways, turning her entire body to do so. Now she no longer made the attempt, ashamed that she had ever felt sorry for herself. Most rooms held patients on respirators. During the long, quiet nights she heard the nurses scurrying to answer the beeping respirators.

"I cried, too, the first time I walked down these halls." Jo handed Maggie a tissue and hurried past a room where a patient was being hosed down on a gurney.

But Maggie noticed and wondered. Bath procedure for quadriplegics?

They returned to Maggie's corner room to find Mike leaning against the doorway and Shelley sitting next to the window.

"You got wheels, Mom," the boy said, straightening and helping his mother to her feet.

"Thank God, they're temporary," Maggie replied. She lay exhausted on the bed. Such little effort, such a meager reserve of energy. "So, how are you two? Where's Kat?"

"At work," Shelley said.

"I'm going for a cup of coffee," Jo announced.

"You want us to go home with you, Mom, and

help take care of you?" Shelley offered. "Or Katherine said you could stay at our place."

Maggie smiled a little grimly. How easy it was for her to forget their rage at her leaving their dad, their resentment when she moved in with Jo, their polite neglect of the past year. Would she forgive them anything? What if one murdered the other? She used to worry about that when they were younger and constantly fighting. But she had taken them from their home, their schools, their friends. There were good reasons for their anger. It was a struggle just to get through the teen years without being disillusioned by one's parents.

"Jo'll take good care of me. But I hope you'll visit whenever you can. I love to see you."

They stood near her bed now, looking distressed. Mike shuffled his feet, his Adam's apple bobbing as he cleared his throat. He frowned and gazed out the window, tongue-tied with youth.

"Mom," Shelley said. "I'll move back in with you if you want."

She studied her daughter. Did Shelley think she would exact such a price from her? "You're enrolled at UW-Milwaukee this fall. How can you?" She turned her eyes on Mike and watched him duck his head. "Look, neither one of you has to do backflips for me. Just don't ignore me anymore. You hear?" They met her smile with their own abashed versions.

"How'd it go?" Jo asked when Shelley and Mike were gone.

"You sure disappeared in a hurry."

"I thought I'd give you time alone. I'm going to do the same when Kat gets here."

Maggie didn't have the energy to argue.

Katherine walked purposefully into the room later in the day. "You could stay with us a couple weeks, both of you," she said. "It's a lot closer to the Medical Complex than Appleton. And there'd be more of us to help."

Maggie felt Jo's eyes on her. "Shelley already offered. I appreciate it, Kat, but I want to go home." It would be more restful being where she belonged. Still, she felt warmed by the invitation.

"Thanks, Katherine." As she left, Jo squeezed Kat's shoulder.

Silence. Then Maggie laughed a little. "Jo's determined to leave me alone with my family."

"Do you want to talk?" Kat asked. She sat in a chair next to the bed.

"Not too long about anything serious, Kat. We'll always be in each other's lives. You know that, I know that. We'll have lots of time to discuss things." Considering recent events, that was probably a foolish assumption. Either one of them could be struck down at any moment. She looked at her sister. Four years separated them. They looked alike, they voted alike, they enjoyed the same books, the same type of music. They differed only in sexual orientation. "Kat, I think I was born this way," she said out of the blue.

"I know, Maggie. I just didn't like being shut out of your life. You weren't honest with me."

"I wasn't honest with anyone." The truth was that she'd felt backed into a corner. Terrified that she might lose her kids if she admitted to her feelings toward women, she'd lied. Her leaving Bill had made no sense to anyone but herself. "I'm sorry."

* * * * *

Wednesday night, Erica downed a glass of wine while awaiting the arrival of Dave's new friend, Steve. She put together a salad, and Dave removed the beef tenderloin from its marinating bag and began peeling potatoes. She felt his gaze and met it with a grin. He was nervous, first slopping the sherry marinade, then sending peelings flying in three directions.

"Calm down, Dave. Once he tastes your cooking, you won't be able to shake him."

"He's probably going to spend the night." He sounded unsure of himself, as if he needed her approval.

She winked. "I'll disappear into my room. I'm tired anyway."

"You don't have to," he said, looking and sounding relieved.

The doorbell rang. Dave jumped. She laughed.

"Just you wait," he warned, wiping his hands on a towel and heading toward the door. "Your turn will come."

With a smile she extended a hand to Steve. He was about Dave's height, wore steel-rim glasses, had a square chin, hazel eyes and light brown hair. She thought him average looking. "Welcome."

"I've been dreading meeting you," he said with a nervous grin.

"Why is that?" she asked, startled.

"Dave made you out to be wonder woman, capable of doing a ten-minute oil change and single-handed tire rotations."

She howled, she liked him.

When they sat down to dinner, they laughed over Steve's youthful efforts to hide his sexuality from his mother. He'd grown up in Indianapolis. "She kept encouraging me to take out the daughter of a close friend. I liked the girl. She was a terrific dancer. We'd go out to eat, go to a gay bar, watch a show, dance a little bit. I'd take her home and go back to the bar and meet someone. We'd end up at his place. One morning my mother said, 'Stevie, you can tell me you like the boys.' When I recovered from the shock, I asked her why she wanted me go out with this girl if she knew. She said, 'To make you tell me.' " He shook his head.

"Mothers are spooky. They always know everything."

"Does your mother know?" she asked Dave, trying to recall how they'd got on the topic of mothers. Then remembered it had to do with coming out.

He shook his head. "I don't think so."

"Ha. I'll bet she does." Steve placed his napkin next to his plate. "What a great meal. Thanks. Both of you."

"Thank Dave," she said. "He's the cook. I'll clean up."

"I'll help," Steve offered.

When they loaded the dishwasher and put the food away, she almost asked him if he did the maintenance on his car. She too could be replaced.

Later that night, she awakened to the sounds of lovemaking. Earlier she had turned on the TV in her room and tried to watch a program on the public television station, but fell asleep in the middle of it. Her window was open. Theirs must be too, she realized. That's why she could hear them, she thought, not because the walls were so thin. One moaned, then the other. She heard the bed springs protesting as they had when she'd made love with Dave.

She found herself stiffening, lying quietly, listening with rapt attention to the sounds they made. Trying to imagine the two men in embrace, she closed her eyes. Turning onto her belly, her hand stole between her legs. She wondered where to imagine herself and with whom and heard herself groan in response to her own efforts. The three of them sounded like a pod of whales, she thought and laughed aloud.

IX

On Saturday morning Jo's mother, Constance McCook, phoned.

"I'm going back to work Monday, Mom. Why do you ask?" Jo said. She stood with one hand on her hip, head down, toe brushing the carpet, listening to her mother. She glanced at Maggie, who, encased in the Minerva cast, was watching from her electric chair. "It's nice of you to offer, Mom. Let me talk to Maggie. Okay?"

"Talk about what?" Maggie asked as she hung up the phone.

"Mom wants to come stay with you during the day next week. I wish you'd let her, Maggie. It would make me feel better and her feel useful."

WELCOME HOME banners still hung from window frames. They had come home to friends, a cake, a dinner. It had felt good. But for the past few days Maggie's hands had been losing feeling. Another worry. Maggie sighed. She didn't like being left alone. When Jo had gone to the store yesterday, she had imagined a man breaking in and assaulting her, breaking her neck again in the process. She'd told Jo about this disturbing image. Jo had said she probably felt vulnerable, unable to run or resist. She wasn't crazy about being trapped with Jo's mother, though, fearing she would talk her ear off.

"What about her crafts?"

"She can work on them here." Jo's mother embroidered and sold framed maxims — *A Man Is Known By The Company He Keeps* — *Take Time To Smell The Roses* — *Live And Let Live* — *Love Is A Two Way Street*. Her creations embarrassed Jo.

"One week," she conceded. "Tell her thanks."

The kids and Kat were visiting today. Maggie left entertaining to others. She made little effort to contribute to conversations unless her kids were around. Then, for some reason, she felt a need to present a good appearance. She coaxed Mike into conversations, softened Shelley's opinions with interpretation. It exhausted her.

Jo coped with company by enlisting needed help. When Mike spent a day or two, she easily talked him into assisting her with projects — stacking wood, moving furniture, cutting tree limbs. She asked Shelley to help fix dinner, to set the table, to clean up afterwards. Kat always offered to assist with anything.

The doorbell rang, the unlocked screen door creaked opened. Maggie heard Kat calling, "Hello the house."

She smiled a little. "Hello yourselves," she called back.

"How are you doing?" Kat asked, encircling her cast with an arm, bending to kiss her.

"Making progress," she replied. Shelley gave her a smacking kiss on the mouth, Mike a shy peck on the cheek. Katherine's lover shook her hand. "Hello, Paul."

"Where's Jo?" Kat asked, looking around.

"In the basement, I think, washing clothes or something."

"You do look better, Mom." Shelley perched on the edge of the couch. She shoved frizzy curls away from her face. Her eyes glowed in the tan of her face.

Comparatively speaking, she supposed she did. But she tired so easily. It worried her. Lately, Nancy had been urging her to cut back on the medication. "I am better. I told my boss to bring me the magazine layout starting September."

Mike hovered nearby. "Think I'll get a Coke."

"Why don't you take orders, Mike?" she suggested, putting her chair back so as to see all of him. He was growing so fast that his parts didn't always look like they belonged together. Right now his arms appeared too long for his body.

"Anybody else want something to drink? How about you, Mom?"

"Just ice water, thanks," she replied with a slight smile. She felt an urgent need to feel close to him, to be an important part of his life once more. But she knew that wasn't possible right now, that it probably never would happen again.

She heard Jo talking to Mike in the kitchen. "Hi, sport, finding what you want?"

"I'm a gofer. That's what happens when you're lowest on the totem pole."

That was a lot of words out of Mike. "I remember. I was the youngest, too. I have three older brothers."

"Wish I did."

"I seldom see them." Jo had told Maggie that she envied her her relationship with Kat, as strained as it had been. It was more than she'd ever had with her brothers. She helped him carry the drinks into the living room and sat down for a few minutes.

Mike appeared uncomfortable. He went to the patio door and stood there, looking out. "Want me to mow the yard?"

"You can if you want." Jo got up. "I'll go with you."

"What'd we say?" Shelley asked. "He's so damn moody."

"You were, too, at his age," Maggie remarked, thinking that Shelley still was.

"He used to talk to me when we lived together." Shelley sounded wistful.

"Oh, honey," Maggie said, almost wishing she could turn back the clock and mend the family break. She wanted to gather Shelley in her arms.

Paul said, "You can probably attribute his moods to raging hormones."

"He's got a girlfriend," Shelley told them.

"Tell me about her." Maggie's interest piqued. She heard the mower sputter to life somewhere out front.

"She's cute — dark hair, blue eyes, petite. Kind of looks like you, Mom. He brought her home when I was at Dad's. She didn't say much." Shelley shrugged.

When they left, Maggie slept for hours.

Early Monday morning, Jo's mother called through the locked screen door, "Anybody home?"

"Just a minute, Mom," Jo yelled from the bathroom and hurried to unhook the screen.

"Hot, huh, Joey?" Her mother kissed her, and she hugged her in return. They stood about the same height, but her mother was heavier. Except for build, Jo took after her father. He too had sandy hair and freckles and gray eyes. Her mother backed off to look at her. "You look nice. You always wear suits to work?"

"Not always, just when I want to impress my mother."

Looking past Jo, her mother beamed. "There's the patient."

Maggie cringed at being called a patient.

Jo's mother said, "I have to go out to the car and get my things. Be back in a flash."

"And I've got to run," Jo said. "Take care, Maggie. If I get a chance, I'll call."

Maggie had dreaded this day — everyone back at

work, herself trapped in the house. She heard two car doors slam, Jo's engine starting, the screen door slapping shut.

"Honey, I'll just sit here on the couch and do my work. Don't pay any attention to me unless you need something. That's what I'm here for." Jo's mother plopped herself at one end of the davenport and reached into the bag at her feet. "Nice music." Mendelssohn's *Italian Symphony* was being played on National Public Radio. "Makes you want to dance."

She found herself smiling. "Mendelssohn's a cheerful composer."

The older woman bent to her work, her glasses nearly slipping off her short nose. "I know Jo doesn't think much of my crafts. That's why I haven't given you any as gifts."

She murmured an unconvincing dissent.

"It's okay. I know this stuff is hokey, but I enjoy doing it and it sells. I don't know why," Constance added with a shrug and then lapsed into silence.

She fell asleep toward the end of the symphony, waking briefly during the morning to see Jo's mother, splashed by sunlight, hunched over her embroidery. She was glad she had not asked Jo to tell her mother she needed silence.

"Time for lunch, honey."

Her eyes popped open when Jo's mother touched her shoulder. Constance set a plate with a sandwich and potato chips on the TV table. Maggie knew she was wet, having just witnessed Gail and Erica making love in a voyeur's dream. Erica had been over yesterday with Gail, bringing a casserole and bread made by Dave. They had stayed to eat with herself and Jo, Nancy and Liz. Slightly disoriented, she momentarily wondered who Constance was and what she was doing here.

Constance leaned over and looked into her face. "Are you all right, Maggie?"

"Yes. Thanks for the food." Seeing some of Jo's caring in her mother's eyes, she was reminded of yesterday's anger with Jo when she had disappeared on a long walk with Gail. Jo had apologized last night, had said she just wanted to get some outside exercise.

Jo's mother sat with her plate on the couch. "Mind if I eat with you?" She wore a pink blouse and slacks, the seams of which strained at the fabric.

She found herself liking this woman. "Of course I don't mind. It's nice of you to stay with me, Constance."

"Well," Jo's mother said between mouthfuls, "I felt so bad about all of this and finally I can do something useful. You know, Jo doesn't like me to interfere with her life, so I try not to." She stopped talking to chew and swallow. "You're a mother, aren't you?"

"Yep. I have a teenage son and daughter."

"I'll bet they're nice kids, too, smart. I have three sons and Jo. She was always special to me and her father, being the only girl and the youngest. I want her to be happy." She shot a shy glance at Maggie. "You make her happy."

When Jo returned from school and Constance left, she told her what her mother had said. She wondered about the truth of it, though, after yesterday. Jo had not seemed happy after the time she had spent alone with Gail.

She had been going to tell Jo about her dream

and scotched that idea, but exciting thoughts kept resurfacing. Maybe she should initiate sex. They had only tried to make love once since she'd broken her neck. It had been difficult for her, strait-jacketed as she was.

Jo grinned and looked embarrassed. "Mom said that, did she?"

"Your parents must know that you're a lesbian."

"I suppose," she said vaguely. "Hungry, sweetie?"

"For you."

Jo looked surprised. "Are you sure?"

Maggie smiled determinedly. "Very sure." Remembering their efforts at manipulation, shortly after their return home from Froedtert, she thought there must be a better way.

"How do we do this?" Jo asked, kneeling before Maggie's electric recliner. "We weren't very successful last time."

"Maybe we have to want it bad enough to be ingenious," Maggie replied, sucking air when Jo slid a hand up the leg of her shorts. "Kiss me."

Jo tore off her suit jacket, removed her skirt and panties and kneeled on the chair. She whispered into Maggie's mouth, "God, you're wet."

Maggie breathed back, "Doesn't it feel good? I'm not going to last long." Then, "Are the doors locked?"

"I don't know and I don't care." She strained against Maggie's hand.

The cast cut at Maggie's armpit, curbing her passion. Jo's muscles closed on her hand as her fingers slid inside on a river of desire. Pulling them out slowly, she teased with long, slow strokes. "You are so swollen."

Jo thrust her tongue into Maggie's mouth and plunged her fingers deep inside. When she withdrew them, she began a tantalizing finger dance.

They were both moving now toward climax. It came simultaneously, something they seldom managed under even the best circumstances.

X

Erica met Gail after work. They played a couple of games of tennis in the September afternoon. It had been a month since she had ridden with Gail to Froedtert. Gail was invited to dinner that evening.

She stood by Erica's car while Erica put away her racket and balls. "I'd like you to move in with me, Erica."

The request was unexpected. "What?"

Gail met her eyes. She looked nervous. "I'm asking you to be my roommate. Will you at least think about it?"

"Why?" She was dumbfounded.

"Because I like you, and it would be nice to share the rent with someone. Please think about it before you answer. Talk it over with Dave."

She did after Gail left that evening.

Dave stared glumly at her. "Isn't this premature? You hardly know her," he said. "Besides, I thought you were just friends."

"I'm bouncing it off you, is all, Dave. Just because I'm talking about it doesn't mean I'm going to do it. And we are just friends. She wants someone to share the rent, not her bed." She didn't really want to move in with Gail. She sensed something between Gail and Jo that shouldn't be there. There was a rubberband effect between them, drawing them together, as if they had never let go. She thought that sometimes Gail used her to annoy Jo.

"So, why move in with her? Save yourself for a lover."

She looked at him and pursed her lips. "What happens when Steve moves in here?"

"Can't we all live together?" he asked, looking troubled.

"Threesomes don't work."

"Sure they do, when the third person isn't sexually compatible."

"I don't want to witness your lovemaking."

"We'll be quiet." He grinned suddenly, causing her to smile. The grin vanished, replaced by a frown. "I don't want you to move out, Erica, not for Steve, not for Gail."

"Don't you like Gail?" They were sitting in the living room.

"I like her all right." He changed the subject. "I was in Hartland's office today, peddling drugs. He's back."

"Yes, I know. Maggie has an appointment with him tomorrow. I'm taking some time off to drive her there. Jo's going to a conference in Madison. The same one Gail's going to, I think."

"Maggie's better, isn't she?"

She thought of the walk they had taken last weekend, to the park and back. Only a few blocks, but nearly too far for Maggie.

Looking out the window, she noticed how dark it was. Despite the continuing warm weather, fall was upon them. The schools were back in session, and her job was demanding.

Maggie met Erica at the door shortly after ten the next morning. "We've got fifteen minutes or so before we have to leave. Want some coffee?"

"I'd kill for a cup." Following Maggie into the kitchen, she thought about how quickly she adjusted to Maggie's changing appearance. The only time she'd seen Maggie without a collar or halo or cast was at the accident site when she'd been rammed head first onto the pavement. Involuntarily, she reached to touch the silken strands of hair that fell over the white cast and, surprised at herself, let the hand fall to her side.

Maggie poured them coffee and took it to the table. "So, what have you been doing?"

"Working." She thought about the problems that

came with being a principal. Some of the difficulties with teachers and students, she suspected, came from the fact that she was a woman.

"Been seeing a lot of Gail?"

She looked at Maggie over the rim of her coffee cup. "Some. We've been playing a lot of tennis, golf on weekends." The exercise relieved some of the work-related stress.

Maggie set her cup down. "I've never seen eyes quite like yours. They're beautiful."

Startled, she felt herself flush. "Thanks." Holding Maggie's gaze, aware of the artery fluttering wildly in her own neck, she felt confused.

Maggie stared back, looking somewhat bewildered herself. Her eyes focused on the blood pulsing in Erica's throat. Her lips twitched a little. She glanced at her watch. "Time to go, don't you think?"

Erica jumped to her feet. "Yes." Her eyes burned and her face was hot.

They said little on the drive to the clinic or during the few minutes spent in the waiting room.

"Why don't you come in with me?" Maggie suggested. "You can help me remember what he says."

Hartland studied Maggie's X-rays, while his nurse helped her sit on the examining table. Pointing a pen at an X-ray, the neurosurgeon told her, "Your neck's fused a little crooked, but that couldn't be helped. They couldn't risk straightening it during surgery. How do you feel?"

Maggie blurted her worries. "My hands and arms often go numb. Sometimes my right leg and foot tingle. If I touch the area around where they took the bone, it's like getting an electric shock."

"Your hip feels that way because the severed nerves are growing back together." He removed the cast and looked at the scar on her neck and the one above her right buttock. "Nice job, hairline scars. The weight of the cast is probably cutting off some circulation to your arms and hands, causing the numbness." He lifted the cast and let it settle back on her shoulders. "Do you need more medication?"

Erica listened. She knew Maggie worried about her prescriptions being renewed. She'd also heard Jo and Nancy urging her to cut back on the pills.

"Yes. When is it going to stop hurting?"

Hartland jingled the change in his pocket and shrugged his shoulders. "I don't know. Bone pain can be difficult to control."

Erica drove her home.

"Can you stay a while?" Maggie unlocked the front door and they stepped into an interior the same temperature as the outdoors.

"I told the secretaries I'd be back this afternoon. I should have taken you out to lunch." Why hadn't she thought to suggest that?

"Nice idea. Maybe we can do lunch in a few weeks. Let's go scrounge in the kitchen for some food."

They made sandwiches from leftover chicken.

Erica carried the food into the living room. "Has your boss brought you any work yet?"

"If you mean this stuff, yes." Maggie gestured at the papers piled on the TV tray next to her. She sighed. "I have a problem hanging onto thoughts, though."

"That'll come back."

Maggie looked at her. "I've been wanting to tell

you that I was lucky when you decided to run that morning. You've been a good friend."

A flush swept up Erica's neck and suffused her face. "I think I'm the lucky one."

It was nearly nine p.m. when Jo walked through the kitchen to the living room.

Nancy and Liz sat side by side on the couch, and Maggie's electric chair had been turned to face the television. "Hi, guys." She set down the book she'd bought for Maggie. "What are you watching?"

"A Kathy and Moe rerun." Nancy glanced at her and turned back to the TV. "It's funny. Come, sit." She patted the cushion next to her.

Jo leaned over to kiss Maggie before settling on the couch next to Nancy.

Later that night, Maggie asked about the conference and Jo filled her in on the details. Jo had been an alcohol and drug abuse counselor for ten years. She counseled adults and kids, gave talks at schools, trained guidance counselors. Keeping a positive attitude toward the future was something Maggie knew she worked at. It frightened her that these kids, some of them with drug- and alcohol-fried brains, were tomorrow's adults, she told Maggie. She lay in bed with her hands under her head, staring at the ceiling. "I asked some of the other people there if they struggle with a somewhat tarnished view of society."

Maggie also lay on her back, the only horizontal

position in which she felt reasonably comfortable. "Didn't the conference run kind of late?"

"I did some shopping and ate supper."

"I never would have guessed by the way you ate when you got home." She reached for Jo's hand, pulling her arm out from under her head. "Thanks for the book. You don't always have to buy me something."

"I wanted to. Tell me more about your appointment. Erica got you there and back all right?"

"Not much to tell. Hartland said my neck's on crooked." Then she had to explain. "I guess I'm lucky it's on at all. People keep pointing that out." It sometimes annoyed her when someone told her how fortunate she was to be alive. She thought she'd been unlucky to have broken her neck at all.

"A few more weeks and you'll be out of the cast."

"Can't be soon enough for me. I've forgotten what a mattress feels like." She, who had always been somewhat claustrophobic, thought she handled being trapped inside the cast rather well. Sometimes she felt like a bug in a jar.

Watching the clock the next day, waiting for Jo to come home, Maggie seethed with anger. Erica, with whom she talked on the phone daily, had said that Gail had been at the conference in Madison yesterday. After hearing that, she had been unable to concentrate on anything. She hadn't been this distressed since before the accident. Maybe it was a sign that she was on the mend.

She heard the van pull into the driveway, the door slam shut, Jo's voice in conversation with someone outside. Then the key turned in the lock and the side door opened. Jo's familiar steps made their way through the kitchen. She watched Jo set her purse on the floor and walk, with a smile, toward her.

"You look decidedly unfriendly, sweetie." Jo leaned over to kiss her. "Something wrong?"

"Gail was at that conference too." Said accusingly.

Jo looked taken aback. "At different sessions."

"Why didn't you tell me she was there?" She studied Jo's reactions.

Jo shrugged. "What's to tell?"

"You had dinner with her?"

Jo answered quickly. "I didn't know she'd be there, and yes, I had dinner with her."

"I don't know why you didn't tell me." Her anger was fading, mirroring her inability to focus on anything for very long.

Wiping her palms on her good slacks, Jo said, "Let me change clothes. Then we'll talk." She went to the bedroom.

Remembering herself with Erica yesterday morning, their daily phone calls, Maggie wondered what made her think she had the right to jump all over Jo. She backed off a little, spent by the anger that had surfaced so suddenly. If Jo was involved with Gail, did she want to know about it? She needed to talk about this with someone. Nancy? Liz? Kat? Erica?

Jo returned to the living room dressed in sweats. Her curls were tousled, her cheeks and mouth ruddy, her gray eyes clouded. She sat on the couch and crossed her arms. "I'm ready."

Maggie looked at her, wondering if she could

forgive Jo for being unfaithful if that was the case. She took note of the stubborn set to her mouth. "So, why didn't you tell me Gail was there?"

"I really didn't know she was going to be there, and I didn't want you upset."

"Don't hide things from me. That makes me angry."

"I won't. I'm sorry." Jo looked contrite. "How was your day?"

"Len picked up the magazine layout today and left me advertising and articles for the next. How was yours?"

"One of the high schools sent me this girl who abuses regularly. I wanted to shake her."

The phone rang. Maggie grabbed the receiver off the phone on the TV tray and pressed it to her cast. Startled to hear her ex-husband's voice, she missed his first few words. "I can't get the phone close to my ear. You have to talk louder," she told him.

He cleared his throat. "When does the cast come off?"

"October twentieth."

"The company's sending me to England for a year. I wondered if Mike could stay with you."

"Does he want to?" she asked, her mind racing ahead for once, digesting this information.

"He doesn't want to go anywhere. His friends and girlfriend are here, but maybe it's good that he'll be separated from her. They're getting awfully cozy." He paused, then added, "We could take him with us, I suppose. That's another option, but he doesn't want to go to England."

"I need to talk about this with Jo. Just the logistics of it. Of course, he can live here. I'd love to have him." Would she? It had been easier without the responsibility of adolescent children. But she loved him and Shelley dearly.

"Oh, and there's Bruno, Mike's dog," he added almost casually.

"Well, guess what now?" she said when she hung up. Jo hadn't moved from her seat. "Bill is being transferred to England for a year, and he asked if we would take Mike and Bruno." She had almost forgotten the dog she'd bought for Mike the day they had gone to the Humane Society a few years back. She had thought he needed a companion. Bruno, a mixed breed, appeared to have mostly black labrador genes. He was large and lumbering, congenial and in love with water.

Jo appeared nonplussed. She sat a little straighter.

"Well, give it some thought," Maggie said, knowing she couldn't turn away her own son.

"It's okay, sweets. I like Mike and I like Bruno." But she sounded hesitant.

"I'm surprised he's not going to live with Kat," Maggie said.

"Maybe he should. Would he be able to attend the same school?"

"No." Already she was mentally preparing a place for him in the house.

XI

Erica rearranged her desktop clutter while waiting for Jonathon Hunter. The sixth grade teacher had been yelling at a student in the hallway. She had heard him when she stepped out of her office. Annoyance gnawed at her. No matter how incorrigible the child, a teacher shouldn't allow himself to be drawn into verbal battles or harangues.

She studied Hunter when he closed the door behind him and leaned against it. School had barely started and already he looked angry, frazzled, as if they were well into the term. She stood up and extended her hand, trying to hide her own frustration, knowing as she did that she was ultimately responsible for his behavior.

He gave her a limp handshake and sat in the empty chair in front of her desk. Leaning forward, his elbows on the arms, he entwined his fingers, pulling at them nervously.

"Tell me what happened, Jon," she began, trying to meet his gaze which was focused on something beyond her left shoulder.

"The boy, Carl Jablonski's his name, called me a fucking asshole. He disrupts class regularly, taunts the boys, teases the girls." His voice rose and the left side of his face twitched a little.

She watched him sympathetically. Some of these kids begged to be punished, she thought. "Why didn't you send him to the office and let us take care of him?"

His eyes met hers briefly, then slipped away. His jaw muscles clenched and his fingers tightened around one another. "He also said I was a fucking faggot."

She felt the force of the words like a slap. "The boy is what? Eleven, twelve? No matter what he says, we can't stoop to his level. Next time send whoever needs disciplining to me."

His lips curled and trembled a little. He was a skinny man of average height, with slightly bulging pale blue eyes. She felt sorry for him until he said, "So he can call you a fucking cunt?"

The words burned through her like an electric current. She stood. "You're saying to me the same sort of things this boy said to you," she snapped.

He got to his feet too. A smile touched his lips

and was gone. "Well, he did call you just that, and that's the kind of mouth he has on him."

Feeling demeaned and defeated, she sank back in her chair for a few minutes, then buzzed her secretary. "Send the boy in." He'd better not call her a fucking cunt to her face, she told herself. She watched him enter the room and stand spread-legged, head thrown back in defiance. "Shut the door, Carl, and come sit down." She gestured toward the chair Hunter had vacated.

"I want my parents here," he said, his fists opening and closing at his sides.

"I want them here, too. Now shut the door and sit down."

He did as she said. When he came closer, she saw the freckles standing out in the pallor of his face. He chewed on his lower lip. "I hate school."

"Is it Mr. Hunter's fault that you dislike school?" She frowned a little at his defiance.

"That faggot. He thinks he can tell me what to do just because he's bigger than me. My dad'll take care of him."

Only his small size made the boy's age believable. There was a menace about him that belonged with someone older. "I've called your mother at work, Carl. We are suspending you for three days. You cannot talk the way you do to teachers. We can't allow you to disrupt class. You'll stay at school until the end of the day."

He jumped to his feet. "Like hell I will," he yelled and ran out of the room.

She went to the door, saw that the vice principal, Phil Steir, held the struggling boy's arms. "We have to keep him here until school ends." She hoped he wouldn't scream any more filth that she would have to act on.

Later she drove home wondering why she had wanted to be a principal. She felt defeated and weary, as if she were somehow less competent than she had been that morning. Opening the front door, she called for Dave, then wandered through the rooms looking for him. She needed to talk. Hearing the front door open and close she hurried to the living room.

"Hi," Steve said, standing just inside the door. She must have looked disconcerted. "Dave left a key under the mat for me." He gestured behind him. "He said he'd be a little late tonight, that you and I should fix a salad. He's going to pick up steaks."

"He didn't tell me," she said, upset at the oversight. Why hadn't he bothered to call her?

"Well, he only told me because I had no way to get inside, unless you were here." Steve smiled nervously. "I feel like a trespasser."

She wanted to tell him that she felt he was too but squelched the words. "How can you be trespassing when Dave left you a key?" she asked sharply. "I'm going to change clothes."

"Me too," he said, holding up his overnight bag.

"Want a drink?" she asked when they met in the kitchen. He wore sweatpants and a T-shirt, she had on shorts and a T-shirt. She took the vodka out of the cupboard and removed a bottle of tonic water from the refrigerator and looked at him. "Guess what I'm having."

He grinned. "Sounds great. Make me a stiff one."

"Bad day?" She poured vodka over ice, filling the

glasses a third of the way. Adding tonic, a twist of lime, a couple of olives, she handed him the drink while swallowing a large gulp of her own.

"Terrible. Yours too?" He swallowed deeply. "Good drink, though. Thanks."

"Mine ended on a very bad note." She met his gaze at eye level. "Why did I ever want to be a principal?"

"You mean it's worse than being a CPA with a nasty boss?" he asked.

They commiserated about their respective employment until Dave walked into the kitchen. He took note of the finished salad and their replenished drinks and stood at the end of the counter dressed in a gray, pinstriped suit. "What gives?" he asked as they stared at him from the table where they sat.

"You better feed us soon," she said.

"You look a little fried. I'll just go put on some other clothes. Don't drink anymore."

Steve squinted at Dave. "Why not? It tastes good, it feels good."

"It ruins your performance," Dave said, loosening his tie and turning his back on them.

She laughed.

Bill was driving Mike and Bruno up from Milwaukee that day, Saturday. So soon, Maggie thought. She hadn't had the energy to prepare his room, which Jo had done, cleaning out the closet and the dressers, even the spare desk. She had asked Jo how she felt about Mike moving back in with them and believed Jo had reneged on an answer. If she were Jo, she wouldn't be happy about living with her lover's teenage son and his huge dog.

What's more, Bill would have to enter the house and talk to Jo, something he had thus far avoided. She couldn't blame him for that either. She still didn't like talking to his new wife, who was at least ten years younger than she was. But then, Jo was about Lacey's age. Were she and Bill clinging to their youth through their partners?

Jo came into the room with an armful of clothes. "We'll have to hang some of this stuff in the basement," she said.

"Need some help?" After all, it was Mike's arrival that was causing all this displacement.

"No, sweetie. You stay put. I don't want to worry about you going up and down the basement steps." Her tone was tinged with annoyance. The front doorbell rang. "Damn." She tossed the coats and jackets she had been carrying onto the couch.

Maggie heard the deeper voices at the door, the brief bark of the dog. Bruno rushed into the living room, his entire body wagging when he recognized her. He whined deep in his throat, bringing tears to her eyes. She tried to pat him as he turned circles under her hands. "Sit, Bruno." He sat on her feet, pressing his quivering frame against her legs, laying his head in her lap. She looked up into Bill and Mike's faces and laughed shakily. "I forgot how big he was."

Mike took the dog's collar, then bent to kiss his mother's cheek.

"Leave him. He's fine." She held a hand out in greeting toward Bill. How strange, even after more than three years, not to kiss him. That would feel natural, she realized. Old habits died hard.

"How are you doing?" Bill asked, looking down at her out of tawny-colored eyes so like their son's. His sandy hair was turning gray.

"Better."

"Quite a cast." His hands rested on his hips as he surveyed her.

"It holds me together." She wondered where Jo had gone, then recalled her snatching up the clothing off the couch.

"Well, shall we get your things, son?" Bill said, turning to Mike. "Where do you want us to put them, Maggie?"

Jo came into the room. "I'll help," she offered.

Bill refused to stay for lunch, saying he had to get on his way, and Maggie breathed relief at his departure. Did she imagine the tension generated by his presence? He had seemed congenial enough, as had Jo.

She was watching Bruno sniff under the bird feeder outside. He had sent the squirrels flying to the tree-tops when he'd rushed out, barking and running in all directions as if he already owned this small piece of earth. Mike was with him, supposedly showing him the yard's boundaries.

Leaning on the back of Maggie's chair, Jo paused in her endless pursuit of order. "Will he really stay in the yard without a fence?"

"Who knows? Mike claims he will. The test will be determined by squirrels, I think."

"Hard to believe he wouldn't chase one into the neighbors' yards. Want me to take Mike and get a video for tonight? To break the ice?"

"Let's ask him. I probably won't stay awake through a movie." She reached for Jo's hand. "Are you going to drive him to school Monday? I called and talked to the administration. His records should be there."

"You can't do it, and it's on my way to work."

There was a feel of fall in the air. Dry leaves, dust, the rapidly fading daylight. Erica and Gail were lobbing balls across the net at the tennis courts near Erica's school when Jo stopped. Getting out of the car, she sat on a park bench.

Gail missed the ball that Erica popped over the net. "Hey, look who's here. You can't count that, Erica. It's Jo's fault." Catching the ball, she walked to the fence, lacing her fingers in the woven wire. "What brings you here?"

"Just passing by."

"Why don't you join us?" Erica jogged to the fence and stood next to Gail.

"I don't have my racket."

"There's an extra one in my trunk," she said, starting toward the gate.

"I have some tennies in the van." Jo went to change her shoes.

They played in the dimming daylight, exchanging partners so that each competed against the other two. Breathing heavily, Jo fell into the fencing in a wild chase after the ball, which had bounced in court on its way out. She slid to the grass. "That's it. I can't run anymore, I'm so out of shape. It's getting too dark anyway. Maggie will wonder where I am."

Gail sprinted over and pulled her to her feet. She said something Erica couldn't hear.

Brushing off her pants, Jo said, "Come see us. Both of you. Mike moved in on Saturday."

"Be right back," Gail said to Erica, walking toward Jo's car with her.

" 'Bye, Jo. Hello to Maggie." Erica was invited over Friday evening, but she wasn't sure Jo knew about the invitation. Opening her trunk, she put the two rackets in and leaned against the Oldsmobile, her eyes on the river across the road from the courts. It flowed away from Lake Winnebago on its journey north toward Green Bay. The bright colors of sunset rippled across its darkening surface. She and Gail were going out for pizza.

It had been a horrendous day. She had met with Carl and his parents at noon, that being the only time they said they could come in. The vice principal and Jon Hunter had been there also. Carl's father, Roger Jablonski, had exchanged verbal unpleasantries with Hunter. The vice principal had calmed them with quiet words: "Let's talk this out. Okay?" His size spoke for him as well, leaving her feeling incompetent once more.

She walked across the road to the edge of the river. Ducks and geese squawked alarm and flew into the water. "Sorry," she said and felt silly, but she hadn't meant to disturb them. Looking over her shoulder, she saw Gail and Jo standing next to the van. If she were Jo, she'd be on her way home to Maggie, not hanging around talking to Gail. Was no one ever satisfied? She felt suddenly irritated and disinclined to wait any longer. Starting toward her car, she called, "Meet you at the Hut."

"I'm coming." Gail hurried to the Probe as she made a U-turn.

Seated at the table near the windows that fronted the city harbor, she eyed the tall masts outlined by the wharf lights. Gail joined her. When the waitress left to get their beers, she studied the meal choices. "What's going on with you and Jo anyway?"

"Nothing," Gail said. "Why don't you come over to my apartment after we eat?"

The waitress set beers in front of them and moved to another table. She sipped through the icy foam and wiped her mouth. "Not tonight, Gail. Thanks anyway."

Gail took a long drink and looked at her over the mug. "I do backrubs."

She smiled. "Another time."

"I thought maybe you could be tempted."

She shook her head and smiled. A sudden image of Maggie's dark, silken hair lying against the white cast flashed through her mind. If Gail were Maggie, would she say no?

When Jo arrived home, Maggie was sitting out back on the small deck, examining a sky littered with stars and galaxies, none of which she could identify.

"Nice night. We won't have many more of these," Jo said, coming outside with a plateful of leftovers. "I saw Erica and Gail on the tennis courts on the way home and played a couple games with them." She pulled a lawn chair close. "How was Mike's first day at school?"

"He said it went okay. It's hard to tell when he's

so uncommunicative." She had to ask questions to get him to talk.

"How was your day?"

"Boring. I'm ready to get this cast off and go back to work. And yours?"

"I saw the girl I told you about again today, the one who's so unappealing. Why I set her up for Mondays, I don't know. It went better, though. She could be attractive if she'd change her expression. I wanted to tell her to sit up straight and stop whining."

"Sounds like you need an attitude adjustment." Maggie spoke into the darkness, wondering if she was annoyed because Jo was late or because she'd spent time with Gail.

XII

On October twentieth Jo took a vacation day from work to drive Maggie to the Medical Complex in Milwaukee. In the X-ray waiting room was a woman in a halo — moving, talking, acting as if she felt no pain, no pressure. Maggie studied her, realizing that halos must work for some people, that not everyone endured the hideous discomfort she had.

During the short time they spent with Dr. Spencer, as he removed the cast and put on the Philadelphia collar, she asked when the pain would go away. She couldn't recall his answer later, or whether he'd given her a reply. He told her to keep the collar on for a month. But, she thought almost joyously, what a minor inconvenience the collar was compared to the cast or, worse yet, the halo. She was nearly free. The bed would no longer be separated from her body by a piece of plastic.

"I can't wait to get in my car and drive," she told Jo, staring ahead at the downpour through which they drove toward home. The windshield wipers beat back and forth monotonously, pushing cold rain toward the edge of their reach where it gathered and rolled away. She felt Jo's glance.

"You shouldn't drive alone yet. You can't turn your head."

That was true, of course, but she'd never be able to turn it very far. She'd have to turn her entire body instead. "I'll use the mirrors."

"I'll worry."

"You've been wonderfully caring, Jo. I love you for it. But can you understand my wanting to go somewhere on my own? Just to the store or to Shopko or High Cliff."

"Not to High Cliff, not alone."

She placed a hand on Jo's thigh and felt Jo's fingers wrap around it. "I'm worried about Mike. He should have friends by now."

Throwing her a brief glance, Jo smiled and squeezed the hand. "He does. He goes around with a bunch of boys."

"He doesn't bring them home." Maggie frowned. "And I'll bet I know why."

"You're probably right, but he'll get used to us."

"Shelley doesn't seem to mind us anymore, anyway." Shelley had spent the weekend with them.

Her daughter, however, didn't have to explain her mother to her friends, most of whom were in Milwaukee. But Shelley had yet to have any of her local friends come over. Instead, she visited their homes. Maggie suddenly felt like a pariah. Should she say something to Mike?

"Let him be, Maggie."

"I will." What good would it do to ask why he never brought anyone home? She couldn't make him give her more than lip-service respect.

Bruno waited inside the door, greeting them as if he had not seen them for days, instead of only this morning. Jo released him into the yard. To their surprise, he seldom strayed onto neighboring properties.

"Mike should have let him out after school," Maggie said, going to the patio door where the dog stood, already wanting to come in out of the rain. Water washed down the expanse of glass.

"How about a fire?" Jo suggested, rolling up newspapers and stuffing them under the grate.

Maggie lowered herself onto the davenport. "Quiet, isn't it? I'm tired."

"It's been a long day for you." Jo placed two pieces of fatwood on the grate, covered them with kindling and logs and lit a match.

Stretching out on the couch, Maggie watched the fire catch. Already she was forgetting to appreciate the absence of the cast. She closed her eyes, surrendering to sleep. In a dream a stern looking Dr. Spencer told her that her neck would always hurt, that she shouldn't be such a sissy, she should stop taking pain medication. Shelley appeared and reminded her mother of her age, that she was too old to cry. But she cried anyway, tears on her cheek. She awoke to Bruno's tongue on her face and sat up.

Bruno turned his attention to the fire, appearing mesmerized by the brightness, the heat and crackling. With a grunt Jo sat on the couch. The three of them stared at the flames licking at the split oak. It felt good to have this quiet moment at home.

As Maggie was relishing the privacy, Mike came in the side door. Bruno rushed to meet him. The boy bypassed the living room and shut his bedroom door on the whining dog.

"Now what gives?" Jo said, switching on the news. The doorbell rang twice and she went to answer it, shushing the dog.

"We're here to celebrate the separation of the cast." Dave waved two bottles of Cook's Champagne.

"We brought dinner too," Nancy said.

Jo grinned as they headed toward the living room. Following, she leaned on the door frame. Mike stood behind her, both of them watching Maggie sit up and stare at the visitors. Erica, Liz, Steve, Gail, Dave and Nancy.

Maggie wore a bemused smile as the house filled with sound. Everyone talking, the dog barking.

The table got set, the food warmed, the champagne opened. They sat down to eat Chinese carryout, passing the paper containers for everyone to sample. Maggie saw Mike go out the side door and looked questioningly at Jo.

Erica was watching Maggie, amazed at the transformation. Maggie's eyes glowed, her cheeks were flushed with heat and excitement, her dark hair glossy in the overhead light. She admired her trim figure, so long hidden by the vest and cast, before asking herself what this was all about. Why was she looking at Maggie's body? Even if she herself was attracted to her, and she wasn't, Maggie was Jo's partner. Once, she pulled her eyes from Maggie and met Jo's measured stare. She looked quickly away.

For no plausible reason, she suddenly pictured Carl Jablonski and his father in this room attacking them verbally and physically. Carl had come back to school after the three-day suspension. Hunter had sent him to her office. And the boy had indeed called her a fucking cunt to her face. She'd had no choice but to suspend him again.

Whenever he returned to school, he immediately challenged authority with obscene language and was once more suspended. Finally, realizing that his intent was to avoid school, she put him one-on-one with a mentor. She worried about Hunter now, his hostility toward the students and herself.

"Erica, are you there somewhere?" Dave asked.

Giving him a slight smile, she realized it was probably Mike sneaking out the door that had brought Carl and Hunter to mind. "I'm here."

As they sat around the living room, talking and watching the fire, the phone rang. The girl Jo found so annoying had been hospitalized following a suicide attempt. She would have to go out into the unpleasant night and talk to her.

Dave got to his feet. "Guess we better leave too. Jo, you don't have to go to such extremes to get rid of us, you know."

Thinking it unfair that the kids who misbehave get most of the attention, Erica stood and stretched.

"We're out of here. We have to get up early tomorrow," Nancy said.

"Don't remind me." Liz yawned.

Steve said, "Never in my wildest dreams did I think I'd enjoy hanging around a bunch of women so much."

Jo shrugged into a raincoat. "Is that a backhanded compliment or what?" She turned to Gail. "Want to play racquetball next week?"

Gail looked startled, then pleased. "Sure. Give me a call."

"You look wonderful, Maggie," Erica said. She was getting used to the hugs that went along with arriving and departing. Feeling the softness of Maggie's body against her own, smelling the good, clean smell of her soap and a lingering scent of unidentifiable cologne, she was surprised by unexpected yearning and backed away. The sight of Maggie's slightly bemused smile remained in her mind as she drove home.

The silence when everyone left filled the room. Maggie fell asleep on the couch and woke when Mike came home. "Where'd you go?" she asked him.

"Out with the guys."

"You could have stayed and eaten with us."

"I know." He sat down with a thump. Bruno pressed against him.

"Mike, your friends are welcome here."

He shot her a furtive glance. "I know. Think I'll go to bed."

With a sigh she decided to do the same.

The cold touch of Jo's skin awoke her. Murmuring a protest, she whispered, "What time is it?"

"Eleven-thirty."

"How'd it go?"

Jo breathed into Maggie's hair. "Not good. She was puking her guts out and resentful as hell. You should see her mother, though. What a sexy woman." She cuddled closer. "Mmm. You smell wonderful. Speaking of sexy women, I almost forgot the feel of your body. How is it without the cast?"

"All those months of looking forward to this and I'm already used to it."

"I'm horny."

"You have to work tomorrow," Maggie said, turning onto her back. She lay very still, savoring the sensation of Jo caressing her breasts, her belly, her thighs.

Jo rolled on top of her. "Am I hurting you?" she whispered.

She murmured no into Jo's mouth as it covered her own. Jo parted her lips with her tongue, her hand closed over Maggie's breast and then journeyed downward over her ribs, her belly, to the merger of her legs.

She stirred under Jo, joining her in a slow, pelvic thrust. Her heart thumped and she wondered why, after so many repetitions, this act still held excitement.

Jo covered the tangle of hair, her fingers penetrating with ease. She shifted her weight a little to one side and thrust deep inside as Maggie rose to meet her.

Inhaling sharply, Maggie wiggled out from underneath. She wrapped an arm around Jo and slipped her other hand between Jo's legs. "You're at sea, darling," she breathed into Jo's mouth, her fingers moving in slow rhythm. How good it felt, making love as they once had.

"I want to go down on you," Jo muttered, her voice thick, almost unrecognizable.

She gave a throaty laugh. "Not until I can. My neck, the collar." Her fingers moved faster, then slowed to tease, then slid inside.

"I can't hold back," Jo whispered, her touch simulating Maggie's.

"Neither can I. I'm just waiting for you."

Long, pleasurable spasms released them from their need.

XIII

Challenged as she often was by Hunter, Erica now dreaded school. Called to his classroom Friday morning, she sat in a back row to observe. There was discussion about moving the sixth grades to the junior high school. That, she thought, would remove Hunter and Carl from her realm.

"Why did you send for me?" she asked when the youngsters left for the gym.

"You couldn't tell?" His eyes blazed.

"No," she said, puzzled.

"They deliberately bait me. That boy at the end of the front row."

"What did he do?" She put her hands in the pockets of her suit jacket. A slight headache plagued her at work and she squinted a little under the fluorescent lights.

"Before you came in he asked why they had to memorize dates. He said he didn't care who did what when in Vietnam. The smart ass. He said we should have bombed the gooks off the earth. Then we wouldn't have them all coming over here."

Appalled, she asked, "What did you say?"

"I told him that all of us came from somewhere else, except the Native Americans."

"That was a good answer, Jon. What do you want me to do?"

"I want you to realize what I'm dealing with here." He was shaking.

"Would you like some time off, sort of a sabbatical?" She touched his arm with concern.

He turned away and thrust his hands deep in his pockets. "You're not going to get rid of me so easily."

She looked at his back. "I'm not trying to get rid of you, Jon. I'm trying to help." A teacher had shot a principal the other day in one of the Milwaukee schools. She feared for Hunter's sanity and for the safety of students, the staff, herself.

That morning Maggie had driven to the store and to Shopko and even filled her car with gas before returning home. She had called Len and told him she wanted to return to work. He had suggested half-days and agreed to her starting Monday. When the phone rang, she was still thinking about that conversation.

"Constance McCook, Maggie. Thought I'd call and see how you were doing."

She smiled a little. "Fine. I'm going back to my job next Monday. By the way, thanks for staying with me that first week Jo went back to work."

"It was nothing. That's wonderful news, Maggie. We'd like to have you and Jo down for Thanksgiving dinner."

"My son is living with us now."

"Bring him along. I know all about boys."

When she talked to Jo during the day, Maggie told her first about her conversation with Len.

Jo was silent a moment before asking, "Are you ready to go back to work?"

"It's time. I don't want my assistant moving into my job." It was early in the day, and she was already tired. She missed the electric chair which they'd taken back to the rental company. "Your mother called. She invited us for Thanksgiving."

"We'll talk about it tonight."

Studying her son over dinner that evening, she asked, "Will you be here for Thanksgiving?" The question made her realize that he had not returned to Milwaukee since moving in with them.

"Yep. I've got practice, which means I'll be late for dinner from now on. I made the basketball team today." Mike looked pleased.

"I didn't know you were trying out."

"Thought I'd give it a go. I'll probably be a bench-sitter for a while."

"Well, that's good, Mike. About making the team. That's wonderful, isn't it, Jo?" she said, searching for the enthusiasm hidden under Mike's cool exterior. "You must be happy."

He grunted around a mouthful of potatoes. Since he'd moved in, their menus were built upon the things he liked — meat, potatoes, salads, dessert.

"Looks like we'll be going to basketball games. When's the first one?" Jo asked.

"You don't have to come." He gulped down his milk.

"We'll want to come." Maggie frowned, hoping he'd want them there.

He shrugged. "I'll get a schedule."

"Let's have Thanksgiving here," Jo said suddenly.

"Your mother asked us there."

"Maybe Aunt Katherine, Paul, and Shelley will come," Mike put in.

Jo smiled wryly. "We'll invite everyone we know."

The boy rolled his eyes.

Monday morning Maggie dressed in a suit. Even if she was only going to work for a few hours, she wanted to look professional. She was nervous, beginning something and then forgetting to finish it. She put bread in the toaster and left the kitchen to apply her makeup.

"Want me to eat your toast, Mom?" Mike hollered from the other room.

"As long as you put in a couple more slices," she said, hunting for the coffee mug she'd put down somewhere. "Where the hell's my cup?"

"Calm down, sweetie," Jo said, kissing her on the cheek. "You look superb."

"I'm trying. I feel like it's the first day on the job."

"Hey, you're good. They've been hanging onto your position all these months. Don't worry."

She parked her Grand Am outside the building, took a deep breath and walked inside. There, hanging in the entryway, was a huge computer-generated WELCOME BACK sign. It lifted her spirits while calming them.

"Good to have you back," Len Brewster said. "Staff meeting in ten minutes."

Her office looked as it had when she left for vacation, except there were roses on the desk from those in the office. During the meeting, her assistant and Len filled her in on what was going on.

She worked on ad layouts until eleven-thirty when she must have looked as gray as she felt, because Len told her to go home. She could continue tomorrow.

Glad she had started back to work for only a few hours at a stretch, Maggie dragged the first week, then began to gain strength. She cut back on medication, taking the pills for pain midday and at night. Although she was exhausted at the end of the days, she felt a deep sense of satisfaction, as if she had won an important contest.

"You beat the odds, kiddo," Nancy told her the

Saturday before Thanksgiving, when she and Jo gave a dinner for their friends who were going to their own families for the holiday.

She removed the Philadelphia collar that day, discarding the last physical reminder of the accident. Another occasion to celebrate. She still felt pain, though, the ache that never quite went away. Mike spent Saturday with friends of his own, the ones she and Jo seldom saw.

Thanksgiving morning she was standing at the stove, dressed in sweats, her hair still wet from the shower, sautéing onions and celery for dressing. No one was expected until noon, when Paul and Katherine and Shelley and Jo's parents were due.

"Smells wonderful," Jo remarked, walking past her with a load of wood.

"You should let Mike do that. Your hair's wet too. What's it like outside?"

"Spitting snow. Hope the roads aren't bad." Jo walked into the living room and filled the wood box. "I like doing this," she called. "Let him sleep."

Setting the finished dressing aside, Maggie went into the living room. Clouds raced across the sky, playing peekaboo with the sun. Light shone through the windows, and she reached over to pet Bruno, who lay in front of the patio doors. She had taken Erica to the airport yesterday afternoon, watched her plane taxi down the runway and felt a sense of loss when the 727 became airborne. She would miss talking to Erica these four days, she thought as she turned on National Public Radio.

"Sit with me," Jo said, patting the floor next to her.

"Why don't we get the food ready, and then we can relax?" She felt restless. It would be nice to have a holiday that didn't require any preparation, when she could pick up a book and read if she wanted or go to a movie. Always there were people to feed and entertain and the television blaring a football game. She didn't understand why dykes wanted to watch a bunch of guys gallop up and down a field, chasing a ball.

Besides, she reminded herself, she was annoyed with Jo, who now played racquetball with Gail on Wednesday evenings. She'd been home late last night, saying they'd had to wait for a court.

Later, as she played Scrabble in the den with Kat and Shelley before dinner, she and Kat alternately crowed and moaned over opportunities taken and lost.

Shelley grinned. "One of these days I'm going to beat you two."

Her mother patted her on the leg. "Sure you are, honey."

"I see you've got your wits back, Maggie," Katherine remarked wryly.

Constance sat nearby, embroidering dishtowels. She had said in greeting, "You look a hundred percent better, honey. Hope you don't mind I brought my work with me. I can't keep up with orders."

The others were gathered in the living room, their voices rising and falling with the action on the TV. The smell of turkey roasting filled the house.

They finished off dinner in less than an hour. Afterwards she said to Jo, "I'm going for a walk with Katherine."

"I want to go too, Mom," Shelley said.

"Not this time." She shook her head, her tone gentle. "You and I'll talk later." She felt guilty about leaving Constance, even though Jo's mother urged them out the door.

Jo warned, "Don't go far and be careful. It might be slippery."

"Always the worrywart," she remarked.

Bruno walked at her side, stopping at every tree to sniff and pee. The sun had dropped far in the west, radiating little warmth in the bleak day. Branches rattled in the wind. She and Kat hunched into their jackets.

"Why'd you drag me out here, Maggie?" Kat asked when they reached the corner and a biting north wind caught them in its pathway. "It couldn't have been just to get out of the clean-up."

She turned her entire body in order to look at her sister. "What would you do if you thought Paul was cheating on you?"

Katherine returned the glance. She frowned.

"Would you confront him with it?" The cold tired her.

"Yes, I would."

"Think about it, Kat. If you ask him and he admits to it, then you have to do something about it. Maybe if you said nothing, it would blow over."

"Are you crazy, Maggie? Fucking around isn't safe

anymore, if it ever was." She gave her a closer, more suspicious look. "Do you know something I don't? Does Shelley suspect Paul is seeing someone?"

"No, Kat." Did she have to come right out and say that she didn't trust Jo with Gail?

"Is Jo cheating on you?" They stood shivering on the street corner, their backs to the wind.

"She spends a lot of time with Gail." She caught a mental glimpse of Erica, turning at the gate to wave. She understood temptation. Bruno was looking back the way they had come, the wind ruffling his coat. She noticed. "I'm freezing too. Let's go home."

The plane dropped out of the sky, wheels locking into place with a thud, air screaming against the flaps. It touched the runway, bounced, the brakes screeched. Shuddering, it slowed and taxied to the small terminal. Erica gathered her hand luggage and climbed down the steps. Braced for the cold, her body resisting the temperature change from Tucson, she hurried to the building with the other passengers.

Waiting inside, Dave put an arm around her and took her bag. "Good to see you, sweetie." He looked grim.

"What's wrong?" she asked.

He shook his head. "Not here. Did you have a good time?"

"Yes. It was wonderfully warm. There were just the two of us, so we didn't go to any great lengths cooking. We went to the Desert Museum, to Madeira Canyon, to this wonderful little town where there were all these artists, Tucumcari or something like that. We talked and talked. My mother asked me if I was gay. Steve was wrong. Mothers don't always know."

Dave winced. "Don't mention his name."

"Oh. Are you okay?"

"I've been better." They waited at the baggage carousel. After a few minutes, the belt jerked to life and Dave grabbed her luggage when it appeared. "I'll get the truck." He dragged the large suitcase to the doors. "What have you got in here? Arizona sand?"

At home he fixed drinks for them both and handed her one.

"Tell me," she demanded.

"I saw him at the bar with someone else. I thought he was out of town."

"Maybe there's a reasonable explanation." She turned up the thermostat. A fire burned in the grate and she stood in front of it, greedily soaking up the heat.

"Yeah. He met another guy. I could rip his nads off. We were just talking about him moving in. Scotch that." He looked at his drink, took a long swallow. "Am I glad you're back."

"I always feel as if I'm in an alien environment out there, on another planet. All that desert vegetation and barren mountains."

He sat on the leather couch. "Tell me about your talk with your mother. She knows you live with me, doesn't she?"

"Yes. She asked me if you were gay."

"What?" he said. "It shows?"

"I never guessed. Remember?" She recalled her

mother's smile when she had stuttered a reply. "I don't know why she thought I was." She looked at him. "Why don't you call Steve?"

"He's been calling. I won't talk to him."

"Oh, Dave, give him a chance."

"I don't want to discuss Steve anymore."

Sitting next to him, she leaned back against the soft leather and ran an appreciative hand over the dark brown arm. "You have expensive tastes."

"I have good taste, except in men," he clarified. "Are you going to Arizona for Christmas too?"

"No. My sister and her family will be with Mom. I don't think I could take even a few days of that."

"Why not?"

"Didn't I ever tell you about Eileen and her husband? They're missionaries. They always try to convert me."

"How depressing. Want another drink? Yes? Stay right there."

She gazed at the flames, wondering how vacation had gone for Maggie and the others, but especially Maggie. She'd had trouble shaking Maggie out of her thoughts, wanting to share every new experience with her. Was her mother right?

XIV

Maggie was glad when the holidays were over. They'd been difficult for her since her divorce from Bill. Not so much this year, though, because Bill was in England so she didn't have to share the kids with him. Still, there was the hassle of finding the right gifts for everyone and the partying that wore her out.

She started working full-time on January second. The pain at the back of her skull had lessened to a dull throb, a presence she thought would always be there. But she had grown stronger with the passing weeks and could stay awake an entire day.

At noon she called Erica from her office. It was when they exchanged news. She leaned back in her chair and looked out the window at the unremitting winter. "How are things?"

"Okay. I just came from the lunch room, where the kids vie to see how far they can throw their food. I wish I could say they shape up when I walk in."

"You're not scary enough, maybe."

"I guess not. Excuse me, Maggie." Erica's voice became muffled, her hand apparently over the receiver.

Swiveling in her chair, she looked out the window and waited.

Erica said, "Sorry. That was the vice principal. God knows what's happening now. How are you?"

"Good. Would you like to go out for dinner Wednesday night?" she asked. Jo would be playing racquetball with Gail. Why should she sit home and wait?

"Love to. What time?"

Erica found the vice principal in his office. "What did you want to see me about, Phil?" She took one of the chairs near his desk.

"Jon Hunter." Phil had put on weight since the beginning of the school year. His neck bulged over the collar of his pink and gray striped shirt, and he looked at her out of deepset eyes. "His wife left him over the holidays."

Her brief euphoria over Maggie's dinner invitation

disappeared. "How's he taking it? Does he talk to you?"

"I heard it from a friend who is a neighbor of his. Apparently Jon and his wife fought a lot and not quietly. Today I asked Jon how he was feeling. He said not good. When I asked what I could do to help, he told me to mind my own business."

She was silent, wondering whether to approach Hunter. He seemed so hostile. "I'll feel him out."

"Good luck," he said drily.

"How's Carl Jablonski getting along?"

"He's not here today."

Terrific, she thought. Soon they'd have to do something about the boy's absences. But discipline was really Phil's job. Let him take care of it. She went to the teachers' lounge. Hunter was not there. She found him sitting at his desk alone in his classroom.

"I just talked to Phil, Jon. If there's anything I can do to help . . ." She left the sentence unfinished.

He gave her a baleful look. "You can both butt out. And don't suggest time off. I know you just want to get rid of me."

Stunned, she stood inside the door. Kids were coming into the room, casting curious looks her way. "I'll be in my office."

Wednesday evening Erica and Maggie met at Chi Chi's. They went into the bar to order margaritas and eat corn chips.

"Nice way to unwind," Erica remarked.

"I suppose," Maggie said absently. She was remembering the terrible fight generated by this evening's plans, fought after Mike had left for school that morning.

Jo had said that she'd probably be home for dinner after racquetball. She'd told her that she was meeting Erica. The dog had slunk around, hiding behind chairs, giving them worried glances.

"What about Mike?" Jo had asked.

"What about him? He can make a sandwich or something."

"Are you going out with Erica just because I'm going to be with Gail? Tit for tat, is that what this is?"

She had given the question serious thought before replying. "No. I like Erica. She's a good friend."

"You okay?" Erica asked.

"Fine." Everything would be dandy, she thought, if she could forget the argument with Jo, Jo's long Wednesday evenings with Gail, Mike's uncommunicativeness. How much of this did she want to share with Erica? Certainly not the stuff about Jo.

"Sometimes it helps to talk." Erica appeared interested, sympathetic.

She found it difficult to talk to Jo lately. Jo had said she obsessed about Mike, had asked her if she really wanted the house filled with hungry teenage boys.

Erica listened, then confided some of her difficulties with Hunter. "It's amazing how many mini-dramas go on every day that we don't know anything about." She refilled their margarita glasses. "Mike's on the basketball team, isn't he?"

She pictured him running up and down the gym,

heard the shouts, the squeaking of sneakers on the waxed floor. He tripped sometimes over his huge feet. "He spends a lot of time on the bench."

"He'll play more when he's a junior." Erica nodded in the direction of a man climbing onto a bar stool. "My problem teacher just walked in. His wife left him over Christmas. Can't say I blame her."

"Maybe we should go eat then."

Erica said a brief hello to Hunter on their way out of the bar.

"Thanks for coming tonight," Maggie said when they were seated.

"I've been looking forward to this, probably more than I should. I like you too much, Maggie." Erica dropped her eyes to her drink. Running a finger around the rim of her glass, she licked the salt.

"I do too," Maggie said softly, warmed by the admission.

Lifting her gaze, Erica looked hopeful. "Really?"

She nodded. "Really."

The waiter set their meals down, warning them that the plates were hot, unwittingly breaking the tense moment.

Before they walked out into the January night, Erica said, "Can we do this again next week?"

"Sure," Maggie said with more assurance than she felt. "Thanks for the nice evening. Talk to you tomorrow." She hoped Mike would be home to act as a buffer.

She found Jo sitting in the living room with him, watching NBA basketball.

Pleased that Mike and Jo were involved in something companionable, she sat down with them for a few minutes. "Did you win?" she asked Jo.

Jo gave her a bleak look. "One game out of three. I'm out of shape."

The look told her that Jo was still angry with her. She turned to her son. "How's practice going, Mike?"

"Okay." His eyes remained glued to the set.

So much for being friendly, she thought. "Think I'll go to bed and read."

No sooner had she slipped between the cool sheets when Jo came into the room and shut the door. "I haven't seen you all day and you say two words and go to bed." Her voice trembled a little.

"You didn't say more than a few words yourself. I thought you wanted to watch basketball."

"I was just passing time, waiting for you to come home from your dinner date. Did you have a good time?" Jo removed her clothes and threw them into the basket in the closet.

"Yes. Did you?" Her tone sharpened. "Erica is only a friend, not an ex-lover."

"Look, it's one thing to play racquetball with an old friend like Gail, quite another for you to seek out Erica's company for a cozy dinner."

Maggie snorted in disbelief. "You think I'm stupid or something, that I believe you spend all those hours on the court." She was breathless, her anger spent. "Are you coming to bed?" Because she disliked going to sleep with unresolved anger, she said, "Look. It can't be all right for you to go out with Gail and wrong for me to have dinner with Erica." Then, realizing she didn't want Jo to say she would give up racquetball with Gail if Maggie would not see Erica alone, she shut up.

They had been talking in fierce whispers. Jo slid

into bed beside Maggie, and they lay stiffly without touching. "We can't even fight right anymore."

"If you mean we can't shriek at each other, that's probably good." Maggie turned her back and burrowed into her pillow. Wind rattled the panes.

"It's supposed to get very cold tomorrow." Jo also turned on her side. Their behinds bumped and they both jumped away from the contact.

"At least twenty below, I heard." Maggie had taken one of her last Halcyon pills and sleep was edging up on her, blurring her thoughts and words.

As the evening replayed itself with remembered conversation and images, Erica tossed restlessly. She couldn't get further than the exchanged confession nor past her own audacity at making it. Now that she'd blurted the words, she knew that she did indeed care too much for Maggie. Was it really possible that Maggie felt the same?

The hum of Steve and Dave's voices in the next room annoyed her as a radio would when turned so low that she could only hear that it was on, not what was being said or played. Dave had forgiven Steve his cheating. When the men's voices faded to silence, she found a restless sleep.

Awakened in the night by snoring, she got up to search for ear plugs and met Dave in the hall. "Can't you make him shut up? Pinch his nose or something?"

Dave crossed his hands over the fly of his Jockey briefs, further irritating her. "He'd probably slug me."

"For God's sake, Dave. How many times have I seen you in the raw?" She wore an undershirt and bikinis and made no effort to cover herself.

"You certainly are crabby," he said. "Are you PMSing?"

Counting a calendar in her head, she snapped, "No, I don't think so. Can we talk?"

In the living room Dave stirred up burning embers in the fireplace and threw on a little kindling and two small logs. "What's going on, sweetie?"

Drawing an afghan around her shoulders, she curled up on the couch. "I went out to dinner with Maggie tonight."

He pulled sweats over his underwear and sat next to her. His hair was tousled, and reflections of the flames leaped in his soft brown eyes. "And?"

"I said something to her that I didn't even know I was thinking."

"Let me guess," he said. "You admitted that you loved her."

"No." Did she love her? Did it show? She told him what had been said.

"It's no surprise to me, sweetie."

"You think my mother was right?"

"Wasn't she?" His eyebrows climbed halfway up his forehead. "Why can't you fall for Gail? Then we can be one big, happy family. I suppose that would be too easy."

She shivered under the afghan. "Just because I really like this one woman doesn't make me a lesbian, does it? Maybe I'm bisexual. I'm not attracted to anyone else."

"Rationalize it all you want, Erica. I could see it

coming. I thought I was bisexual too. Now I think it's just a step on the way to admitting you're gay."

"Why didn't you warn me?"

"I thought maybe this thing with Gail would grow." He smiled sleepily. "We have to work tomorrow."

"I can't sleep with him snoring."

"I'll make him turn over or something."

XV

Twelve inches of snow fell on the ten inches already on the ground toward the end of the second week of January. Jo and Mike shoveled as it continued falling Friday night. Maggie swept behind them for a short distance as an excuse to be outside. She loved the snow, but it was too cold to be out in it for long. A hush had settled over the city, broken only by occasional vehicles whirring by, shovels scraping on pavement, snow blowers clearing sidewalks and driveways.

"A snowblower should be your next purchase," Mike said, his breath a frozen cloud around his head.

"I'm thinking about it," Jo acknowledged into her muffler.

A deep freeze had set in. Temperatures twenty to thirty below zero gripped the state with wind-chills dipping to minus seventy and eighty. Vehicles refused to start. Batteries died. Gas lines froze, stopping traffic in its tracks. Schools closed. Tonight's basketball game had been cancelled.

Maggie and Jo put Heet in their vehicles, kept their tanks full, ran their engines until the thermostat registered normal. Maggie carried an extra key and locked the doors while the Grand Am purred, shrouded in exhaust fumes. She knew Jo worried about her.

She went inside when she was thoroughly chilled. It was too cold to even have a fire, because the thermostat would warm up and shut off the furnace and the rest of the house would quickly turn cold.

The best thing to do was go to bed and huddle with the electric blanket on. It was even too cold for sex. The need to be inside was giving her a bad case of cabin fever.

Temperatures moderated to fifteen below on Wednesday and the schools reopened. Erica had been at work the days the building was closed, huddled in her office with a portable heater at her feet because the thermostat was turned to its lowest setting. Phil, the vice principal, came in both days too for a few hours at a time. He said that Hunter was behaving bizarrely. Jon's wife had told the wife of Phil's friend that her husband was harassing her — calling her constantly, following her around.

Phil had said, "I hate to say this, but he's a dangerous man."

The halls filled with shouting, shuffling children. The bell clamored, signaling the beginning of classes, the closing of doors, the muffling of voices except those raised in play from the gym. She realized she had missed these sounds the past two days, that she actually liked the school atmosphere. She stood outside the office door for a few moments, listening.

She and Phil had scheduled a meeting on teacher morale after school. They discussed the agenda in her office toward the end of the day. "This is a big, empty place without the kids," she said.

"I think the community ought to make better use of these buildings, that they should be opened for other events when school is out."

She agreed. "There's always the liability issue, though. The whole country is sue-crazy." She smiled at him. "And I think we're ready to face the faculty."

The buses carried away their cargos of kids, leaving the halls once again quiet. Her footsteps and Phil's echoed on the tile floor. Chairs scraped in the cafeteria as the teachers gathered, their voices loud in the large room. The weather was the main topic of conversation. Whose vehicles had died in the bitter cold. Whose pipes had burst.

When they quieted, she said, "This is your meeting. You tell Phil and me your concerns, your needs, so that we can provide a healthy environment where kids can learn." She had been a teacher once, wanting a workplace that fostered harmony among the faculty. Turning to Phil, she said quietly, "Jon Hunter's not here."

"I'll go look for him."

The teachers started throwing suggestions at her. They needed to feel that she and Phil would back them up when it came to dealing with disrespectful students and angry parents. She jotted notes, hoping that Phil would hurry back with Hunter. Jon needed to be part of this discussion, so that he didn't fling a wrench into the resulting decisions.

Phil returned alone, looking worried. He whispered into her ear, "His room is a mess."

After the meeting, they went to Hunter's empty classroom. Looking for a clue to the sixth-grade teacher's state of mind, she studied the unwiped slate board, found it scribbled full with equations and historical names and places. Student desks were overturned at random. She noticed Phil trying to force open Hunter's desk drawers. Because regular classroom doors were unsecured, teachers often locked their desks. There was always the threat of vandalism.

She closed the door. "What are you doing, Phil?"

"I think we need to search his desk before something happens." He continued his efforts.

"Before what happens?" Goose bumps galloped up her spine.

"Bingo," he said with satisfaction. The middle drawer opened and he shuffled through the contents. He held up what looked like a box of staples. "This is what I was afraid of."

She stared, then moved close enough to identify the box as ammunition. She met his troubled gaze with her own. "Can you jimmy open the other drawers?"

They found nothing else. Phil handed her the container of bullets and closed and locked the desk. They walked silently back to their offices. Hunter would have to be confronted.

"I think we're going to have to bring in the superintendent and the union rep when we talk to Jon tomorrow," she said.

He nodded. "I agree."

She and Maggie had called off their dinner plans tonight because of the continued cold. She had been surprised at the emptiness she'd felt when she talked to Maggie on the phone at noon. The seven days between now and next Wednesday loomed like an interminable space of time.

At home that evening, she played Spite and Malice with Dave to pass the hours. As she told him her fears and worries about tomorrow, she repeatedly forgot to play the cards on her pile. Dave won easily.

"Come on, sweetie. Pay attention. It's no fun beating you when you don't care."

She dreaded the morning when she'd have to face decisions impacting on Hunter's future. She'd suggested to the superintendent that Jon be asked to take a leave of absence and get counseling. If he refused, she wanted his resignation. It was the confrontation she feared.

"Sorry." She gave him a troubled look. "Do you have anything to make me sleep?" He always carried drug samples to leave in doctors' offices.

"I should have something in my briefcase."

The next morning she was sorry she'd asked for a

sleeping aid. Dave pounded on her door, when public radio's *Morning Edition* failed to wake her. She felt drugged and couldn't wait to crawl back into bed that night.

Phil was already at school when she arrived. She'd been lucky to reach the superintendent before leaving her office yesterday. The union representative was not located until the morning. A substitute, who had been called to take Hunter's class, waited in Phil's office. Everything was in place.

She met with the superintendent, Bruce Livingston, the union rep, Linda Bender, and Phil. They discussed the situation before asking one of the secretaries to go to Hunter's room with the substitute.

Momentarily panicked by the scenario she'd set into motion, she felt her thoughts scatter as she looked around the room. She could not tell what Livingston was thinking. A forbidding man, he'd seldom shown her a smile. He sat next to her desk, facing the door, his arms and legs crossed. Bender took the chair on the other side of the desk, her legs crossed. There was a certain self-assurance about the union rep that made her think Bender was gay. She couldn't have explained why.

Phil broke the tense silence. "We have pretty good teacher-student morale here."

Startled, she smiled tensely. She realized he was trying to bolster her position. But it only made her wonder if her job performance needed defending. The door was open. She would hate to be Hunter, having to walk into this room.

When he did, he did it with moxie. He closed the

door and leaned against it. His eyes looked wild, his pupils huge. "Someone broke into my desk last night."

"I did," Phil said quietly, holding up the small box of bullets.

"Why do you have handgun ammunition at school, Mr. Hunter?" the superintendent asked.

Sitting behind her desk, Erica wondered if she should instead be diving for cover.

"Is that a crime?" Hunter looked at the union rep. "Are you going to let them get away with this?"

"You may ask for representation, Jon," Bender replied.

Livingston began to talk. "Ms. Young and Mr. Steir told me that you've been under a lot of stress, Mr. Hunter. We think it best that you take a leave of absence for the rest of the year. We also believe that counseling would be helpful. If you resolve your problems, we will agree to consider your reinstatement next fall."

Hunter glowered at them, then thrust his chin at Erica. "She's been trying to get rid of me for a long time."

"I think this is a fair solution all the way around," she said.

"And if I don't agree with your fucking solution?"

Shocked that he would use damning language, she had the frightening feeling that Hunter didn't care what happened to him, which would make him a dangerous man.

She heard Livingston say, "Then we'll have to ask for your resignation."

"I quit," Hunter snarled. He left them all standing as he slammed out the door.

"Well," she breathed into the quiet, "so much for that." She glanced at Phil. "He might go to his room and clean out his desk."

"I'll go with him." He left the room.

Livingston shook her hand. "I hope this marks the end of a problematic situation. The man is obviously unstable."

She was alone with Linda Bender. Their eyes met.

Linda gave her a faint smile. "This was a no-win situation. You didn't hire Hunter, did you? No?" She gave her a firm handshake. "Don't think of us as on opposite sides of the fence. Okay?"

She nodded, liking the woman.

The following Wednesday, Maggie left Erica at the restaurant around nine-thirty. They'd given up waiting for warmer temperatures. Thermometers had registered fifteen balmy degrees over the weekend. Now they were back in the cellar with daytime highs hovering around zero. Exhaust filled the air. Snow crunched under the wheels of her car, and clods of ice bounced off the undercarriage.

Turning onto Bluemound, she thought she'd take the BB entrance onto Hwy 41. She'd forgotten that Gail lived just off Bluemound and was genuinely surprised when she recognized Jo's van pulling into traffic a half block in front of her. After checking out the license plate, she slowed to put distance between her own Grand Am and the Caravan.

Instead of turning west on BB as Jo had, she turned east toward town. At home before it seemed possible, she parked in the garage next to Jo's steaming van and sat for a moment in the car. She felt physically ill. She hadn't expected to beat Jo home and needed the time to digest what she'd seen. Now she had to decide how to deal with the information.

Mike was in the living room watching basketball. He grunted a hello.

"Did you find something to eat?" She shrugged out of her coat and hung it in the hall closet. "How was practice?"

"I made a couple sandwiches." He gave her a friendly look. "Coach said I might start on Friday."

"That's wonderful, Mike. I hope the game's at home." He nodded and she dropped a kiss on his forehead. "Where's Jo?"

"In the bathroom." He turned back to the TV.

Where else? Washing off the remains of Gail's scent, no doubt. She went to the bedroom to change her clothes, thinking she would read in bed a while. How she felt when she saw Jo would determine what she said about tonight.

"Hi, sweets." Jo smiled tensely. She wore her nighttime attire of undershirt and bikinis and smelled of cologne.

"Perfume? At night?" she inquired, looking up over her reading glasses. She dropped her book on the floor and scooted down under the covers.

"You're not going to read?" Jo asked as Maggie cuddled close. "Aren't you tired?" She reached up and turned off the light clamped to the headboard.

"I think I've just come to life," she remarked, caressing Jo.

"It's after ten."

Her hand rested on the wiry mound between Jo's

legs. "It's not like you to say no." She slipped her fingers under the elastic leg band.

Jo faced her and drew her tight against her body. "Let's plan an early bedtime tomorrow." She kissed her hair. "Mmm, you always smell so good."

She let it go. Jo had failed the test. Did she really want to force Jo to go from Gail to herself? Her suspicions held her heart in a painful, breath-taking grip. They also made her angry.

Lying awake, listening to Jo's even breathing, she recalled the evening. She and Erica had discussed work and steered away from anything that might hint of intimacy. But the attraction was growing. She was sorely tempted to allow it to blossom, in light of what was going on with Jo.

In her mind's eye, she saw Erica. The thick, blonde hair that nearly reached her shoulders, the electrifying light blue eyes, the enviable figure that most women would give their eye teeth to have. Tonight she'd found herself staring at Erica's hands. They were large and capable-looking, and she had briefly imagined how they would feel on her body.

At dinner the next night, they listened to Mike talk as if watching a transformation. He was telling them about a teacher, a Mrs. Hunter, while Maggie tried to place where and why the name sounded so familiar.

"She teaches English comp. She knows her stuff, but she's weird."

"Why is that?" Maggie asked.

"She's got this nervous twitch, and she's so

jumpy. There was this noise in the hall today, like somebody dropped their books, and you'd think she'd been shot."

Erica had told her about the confrontation and Hunter's quitting. Maybe this woman teacher was his wife. "Is she married?"

"She used to wear a couple rings. I remember because one was this dinky diamond that you could hardly see. She's left-handed and she'd run a finger over the mistakes on your papers. The rings were gone after Christmas when she gave me back a story she made us write."

"What'd you write about?" she asked.

He shrugged and lapsed into reticence. "I don't remember. Bruno, I think."

"Will you show it to me?" she persisted.

"I threw it away. Got a B, though."

She hid her disappointment. "You are getting good grades, Mike."

"Have to. Coach won't let us play otherwise."

She looked at Jo, who raised her eyebrows in unspoken communication. In apparent response to his name, Bruno placed his head on Mike's lap. She didn't have the heart to tell the dog to go lie down. He was not supposed to hang around the table while they ate.

"I'm going to give a talk at your high school next month," Jo told Mike.

Maggie asked, "What about?"

"The usual. Drug and substance abuse. The district principals and superintendent and junior high as well as high school students will be at the assembly. I'm not the only one going to speak.

Someone from Human Services will talk about depression. Should be interesting."

Erica would be one of the attending principals. All day Maggie had pondered Jo's possible infidelity. She'd found herself staring at advertising and articles and seeing instead Jo and Gail in compromising positions. It had made her feel sick.

"I'm going to the library tonight. Hunter wants a resource paper this time." Mike was finishing up the meal with a huge bowl of ice cream.

"Need a ride?" she offered.

"Nope. T.J.'s picking me up." He started toward the kitchen with his dishes.

"T.J.'s old enough to drive?" She knew he was a sophomore.

Mike laughed. "He got held back a year."

She glanced at Jo and caught her wink and grin. She'd forgotten about Jo's promised early bedtime tonight. Maybe she could finagle a backrub. Her neck and back ached from bending over layouts.

When Mike left, Jo asked, "Ready?"

"I wish he'd tell his friends to come to the door, instead of blowing their horns."

"Who cares, Maggie. We have a night alone. Let's take advantage of it." Jo stood behind her as she loaded the dishwasher.

She felt Jo's arms encircle her and she stiffened. "I'm tense and sore."

"Come on, I'll give you a massage first."

She realized that, in spite of everything, she was in the mood. She sometimes wondered at her desire which surfaced without warning. She had always been at the mercy of her own passion.

XVI

Maggie and Jo had gone to every one of the boys' home basketball games so far. They always sat as close to the middle and the floor as they could. Friday night Mike had told them he might start, so they got there early to get a better seat.

The benches were hard. Maggie put her heavy jacket under her and sat down only a few rows behind the home team. When the band played the school song, the players ran onto the floor and began practicing at one end of the gym.

She watched Mike line up as his teammates took turns dribbling to the basket and shooting while another player acted as guard. He didn't look into the bleachers to see who was there. She cheered wildly when he made a practice basket and could have kicked herself when she thought he blushed.

Jo grinned at her. "Hey, Mama, getting a little excited already? The game hasn't started yet."

She flushed and smiled sheepishly. "Can't help it. I get carried away."

The stands were filling with students and parents, jostling them as they settled in. When the school band played the national anthem, everyone stood with hands on hearts and sang along. She felt like a high school student all over again.

When the boys broke from their huddle, the starters running to the center line, she shouted and clapped. Mike readied for the tip-off, bending forward, his knees flexed, his arms hanging loose, ready to run with the ball or act as guard.

He got the ball and dribbled it down the floor, and she leaped to her feet and yelled. He tripped and an opposing player bounced the ball out of his hands. She sat down, disappointed for him and wondering if she was an embarrassment.

"You think he knew it was me?" she asked Jo.

Jo looked amused. "Cheer when he makes a basket or steals a play. Then you won't have to worry.

Mike made three baskets and two free throws and was benched after four fouls. The fans gave him a hand. Before he sat down, he scanned the stands, found his mother and Jo and grinned.

The brief acknowledgment made her heart leap with joy. "Did you see that, Jo?" she said in a voice hoarse from shrieking.

"Yes, Maggie. That was nice."

On the way home she wondered why a little deserved attention from her kid should make her wildly happy.

Dr. Spencer had told Maggie that she could cross-country ski six months after the fusion. On the afternoon of the third Sunday in February she and Jo, along with Nancy and Liz, drove to Hartman's Creek. The sun glowed out of a cloudless sky. Temperatures had already reached the high twenties.

They were starved for fresh air and sunshine and took to the woods and hills along with a host of other skiers. Over thirty inches of snow blanketed the ground, and the ski tracks were deep from constant traffic.

She thought she had shed physical fears with the accident, even going so far as to say to Jo, "You never know what's going to happen, so why worry?"

Now she watched Jo, who was following Liz and Nancy, disappear around a bend in the trail. She didn't try to keep up. The idea was to be outside and enjoy the scenery. Skate skiers passed her, flourishing their skis and poles in her face. Other diagonal skiers stepped out of the tracks and left her behind. She puttered along, listening to the chickadees and nuthatches and bluejays. Once she saw a flash of red and recognized the call of a cardinal. Coming around a curve, she noticed Jo and Nancy and Liz waiting at the top of the next hill.

"You okay?" Jo shouted.

She panted as she duck-walked her skis up the incline. Her legs felt rubbery. She'd gotten little exercise during the frigid spell. Her good intentions to take Bruno for long walks had gone unfulfilled. "Yeah, I'm fine," she hollered. "Just out of shape. You go ahead and let me take my time."

At the top of the hill she rested. The others were out of sight, and she eyed the downgrade with trepidation. The trails were wide enough, but this one was steep and had a curve halfway down. She didn't have the control over these skis that she did over her downhill skis.

A couple topped the hill behind her and she stepped out of the tracks. They greeted her and pushed off. Well, she could do that too. What was she waiting for? Putting her skis back in the tracks, she used her poles to give her momentum.

Maybe she was too stiff, unable to limber up enough to distribute her weight for the turn. Plowing out of the tracks and into the snowbank, she landed with a thump on her tailbone. She felt the jarring in the back of her head. It scared her, a harsh reminder of what there was to fear. Her timidity shamed her.

While she waited in the van, she thought about her unwillingness to tell Jo that she had seen her van near Gail's apartment complex Wednesday night. She didn't understand it. For all she knew, Jo had driven Gail to the Y and back again. Maybe Gail's car had broken down during the cold.

An hour passed before the other three walked

toward the Dodge carrying their skis and some of their outerwear. They had shed hats and gloves and jackets.

"Been waiting long?" Jo asked as they loaded the van with their gear.

"A while. I got tired. Good thing I brought a book."

"Some of those hills were pretty steep." Nancy pulled the side door shut behind herself and Liz.

"Don't I know," she said drily.

Jo slid behind the wheel and turned. "You fell?"

"Yes."

"Were you hurt?" Jo's eyes darkened with concern. "We shouldn't have come."

"I'm fine. Honest."

"Let's go to the Wagon Wheel for pizza." Liz leaned forward and squeezed Maggie's shoulder. "I think you're really brave."

Erica skied with Gail over the weekend at Winter Park near Minocqua, staying two days and a night. Over the phone Monday at noon she told Maggie about their trip.

Maggie listened without comment, then added her weekend news. "It felt good to be outside, didn't it?"

"Are we meeting for dinner Wednesday?" Erica asked, turning her chair around so that she could look through the window at the snow-covered school grounds.

"Where do you want to go?" Then, "I forgot to tell you that Mike's English comp teacher is named Mrs. Hunter."

"Really?" she said, thinking what a difference Hunter's departure had made. Her job was actually enjoyable. "That could be Jon's wife. I don't know."

Maggie related Mike's observations about the English teacher. "Do you think she's afraid of him?"

"Maybe. Or perhaps she's just a nervous person. I sometimes wondered when Hunter was in my office whether I should dive under my desk." A slight exaggeration. She hadn't taken her fleeting anxieties about Hunter being dangerous very seriously.

"Jo's giving a talk at Mike's school next month. I understand the district principals and superintendent will be there."

"Yes. I'm looking forward to it. How is Jo?"

"Okay. How's Gail?"

"Fine, I guess." She paused, then said, "Gail and I are just friends, Maggie."

"That's none of my business, Erica. Want to meet at Victoria's Wednesday?"

She spoke in a rush. "Why don't you come to my place? Dave will be out of town Wednesday and Thursday."

"Can I bring anything?"

"Just yourself." Erica hung up and took a deep, shaky breath. It was done. If something happened, then it did. Anything was possible. Her thoughts turned to dinner. She wanted it to be special, but it was Dave who made the culinary delights. She had two days to come up with a menu. Maybe Dave would help.

"You're playing with fire," he warned her that night as they sat at the table. Rarely now did they have an evening alone.

"Where's Steve?" she asked.

"It's not my day to watch him." He filled her wine glass.

"That's enough." She covered the glass with her hand. "Will you help me with this dinner?"

"I won't be here."

"We can prepare it Tuesday evening," she pleaded.

"You do this often and you'll end up in the sack. Is that what you want?"

"Why do you think everyone has to end up in bed?" Not her, she told herself. She wouldn't risk losing Maggie that way.

"Because that's what happens." He passed her leftover lasagna.

"Is Steve out of town?"

"We had a fight Sunday. He wants to date other men."

"What if he doesn't use condoms, Dave?" What if one broke?

"That's what the fight was about, Erica. I don't always want to have safe sex." He sighed.

"Don't take chances," she begged.

"If I was HIV positive, what would you do?"

The question took her breath away. "Take care of you, if you'd let me. What would you do?"

"Get in my car and drive someplace warm." He smiled. "I'll help you fix a gourmet feast."

"She'll know I didn't do it myself."

"Okay. We'll plan an easy-to-fix meal."

Apprehensively awaiting Maggie's arrival, Erica now wished that Dave hadn't gone out of town, that he would be joining them for dinner. He'd suggested a chicken stir-fry, something he was sure would cause her no trouble. She could prepare it under Maggie's eyes and then Maggie would know that it was her doing. As if Maggie would care, she thought as she sliced onions and peppers and cabbage.

When the doorbell rang, she jumped — just as Dave had done when Steve came to dinner that first time. It made her smile.

A rush of cold air ushered Maggie inside. "A bit brisk out there."

"Damp," she said, taking Maggie's coat. "Did you come from work?"

Maggie nodded. "I stayed late."

"Jo and Gail have a contest going, I hear."

Maggie hadn't heard.

"Whoever wins ten games takes the other out to dinner." She saw the flash of anger on Maggie's face. Maybe it was best not to mention Gail and Jo in the same sentence.

Maggie looked around the room. She had only been in the condominium once. "This is nice. How are Dave and Steve?"

"Dave's fine. I haven't seen Steve for a while. I don't know what to think, not that it matters." She told Maggie about Steve wanting to see other men. "Come on into the kitchen."

Maggie followed her. "Sounds a little dangerous these days."

"I know." She didn't want to worry about Dave right now. "You can talk to me while I get dinner ready."

"Can I help?" Maggie stood nearby.

"Sure." She found the other cutting board and a knife. "Dave thought I could handle a stir-fry," she said with a grin.

"You don't like to cook?" Maggie diced alongside her.

"I'd rather do other things, and Dave loves to cook." She smiled. "I see Mike got eight points Friday night. That's a good start." She'd read about the game in the local paper.

"I shouted myself hoarse. He's loosening up on the court and at home. He brought his friend T.J. to the house Saturday morning and introduced him."

Maggie sautéed the vegetables while Erica started the rice and popped the rolls into the oven. Then Maggie set the table and stood by, watching her finish the meal.

"This okay, coming here tonight?" she asked when they sat down to dinner.

"I have to confess I didn't tell Jo we were eating here." Maggie looked troubled.

"Why? Does she object to our going out to dinner on Wednesdays?" She paused with a forkful of food poised in mid-air.

Maggie met her gaze. "She has no right to, does she? She's with Gail those nights." She smiled and lifted her glass of wine in a toast. "Good food."

"Thanks. You helped fix it."

After they'd cleaned up, Erica lit a fire in the living room fireplace, then sat on one end of the davenport while Maggie took the other.

They watched the flames take hold. "I've about had it with fires this winter," she remarked, looking at Maggie. "I'm ready for spring."

"Think it's ever going to come?" Maggie murmured, meeting her gaze.

It was Erica who made the first move. Later, she would wonder at her own audacity, since she had never approached a woman sexually. After, she would swear that she'd never intended to come on to Maggie. It felt like a dream, something she only imagined.

She moved closer after adding a log to the fire.

Maggie gave her a nervous smile. "Erica..." Maggie's eyes focused on her throat. She must have guessed what was coming.

Erica said nothing. Just leaned forward and tasted the sweetness of Maggie's mouth. Inhaling the scent of Maggie's skin, her hair, her cologne, she wrapped her in her arms and drew her close. She hugged Maggie until she heard her breath catch, then loosened her hold. It occurred to her that when the kissing stopped, she'd have to say something. Somehow, though, this all felt natural.

When she drew Maggie down on the leather couch, she somehow lost control over the situation.

Suddenly Maggie was on top and she wasn't quite sure how they'd changed positions. Her heart pounded in her chest and throat, and she struggled to breathe. She felt Maggie's tongue in her mouth, her hand enclosing her breast, then covering the dampness between her legs. She thought she might drown in sensation.

Maggie's husky laugh sent shivers up her spine. "If we're going to do this, let's get comfortable."

"You want to go to my room?" Her own voice sounded thick, breathy.

"If we're going to finish..." Maggie nodded. She was poised above Erica, her eyes hooded and dark. She lifted herself to her feet.

Erica got up and rearranged her clothes. She stood a good head above Maggie. "Yes," she said as if to herself. But once in the bedroom, she became self-conscious and a little panicky. "I didn't plan any of this, Maggie. I don't want to lose you as a friend."

"Let's not talk about it." Sitting on the bed, Maggie watched her pull her sweater over her head. When she reached behind with both hands to unhook her bra, Maggie said, "Let me." Clasping the freed breasts, she bent to kiss them, then traced the blue veins with a finger. "They're beautiful," she whispered.

Hardly able to catch her breath or move, Erica stood transfixed. Maggie was working her jeans and panties over her hips and down her legs, kneeling to kiss the mound of blonde pubic hair.

When Maggie started to jerk her own sweater off, she took over, then looked shyly at Maggie's nakedness. She found she couldn't speak and almost reverently covered the small, firm breasts with her hands.

She discovered her voice when Maggie turned toward the bed. "What a cute butt."

Maggie laughed. "Yours is magnificent."

"Magnificently large."

They lay together on the sheets. "You're perfectly proportioned. Did anyone ever tell you that?" Maggie asked.

She shook her head. "Nope. Did anyone tell you that you are too?"

"Yep. A woman." Maggie leaned over her and

brushed her face and neck with kisses, took her nipples to suckle. Placing a hand on the tangled mound of curls, Maggie worked her fingers inside.

Erica had never experienced such all-consuming desire. She felt herself riding the edge of climax, a long, exquisite ache. Her lips touched Maggie's.

Occasionally they kissed as they uttered small cries of ecstasy into each other's mouths. Anchored together with an arm, each used her free hand to coax pleasure from the other. Their hands and bodies moved in the quickening rhythm of a sexual dance, which ended abruptly in the surging contractions of orgasm.

They lay quietly then, realizing what they had done.

"Jo's cheating on me," Maggie murmured.

"I'm sorry, Maggie," she whispered, but she wasn't. She hungered to do it all over again.

XVII

Looking at herself in the bathroom mirror, Maggie saw nothing different. She hadn't expected to look changed. When she had been in her teens, she had watched her parents carefully to see if she could determine when they had made love. She had thought to see them altered somehow by the act, but she'd never been able to detect differences in the way they treated each other.

Putting the lovemaking with Erica into a separate category, not to be examined against her feelings toward Jo, she thought she could keep the two events out of conflict. She was acutely aware of the debt she owed Jo for her caretaking, never mind that she suspected Jo of faithlessness herself.

But then, she had once accrued an obligation toward Bill, too, for all the years and ties between them. They had established credits of kindnesses toward each other, which had been undercut with lies and infidelities. He had fallen in love with Lacey. She had discovered her sexual feelings toward women.

She could never bear to think about her separation and divorce very long. It made her too sad. Would she also be looking back on her relationship with Jo with regret in months to come? Could anyone build success on failure? Or was unfaithfulness simply a catalyst to bring on change in a relationship? Her counselor after the separation had put that idea into her head. She never would have thought of it herself.

A knock on the door. "Hey, Mom, did you drown or something?"

"I'll be out in a minute." She turned sideways and examined her stiffness in the mirror. Her neck ached if she attempted to turn it very far. Even though she had been told that the turning radius of her neck would be very limited, it always surprised her to see how much movement had been lost.

Half asleep when Jo climbed into bed with her, she turned away.

"You awake, Maggie?"

Maggie grunted.

Jo curled her body around Maggie's back, put an arm over her and cupped a breast.

* * * * *

157

Erica sensed Maggie distancing herself. Their phone calls became impersonal exchanges of information. With difficulty she accepted the subtle change in their friendship. She had overstepped the bounds. She only hoped that Maggie wouldn't move entirely out of her life. Despairingly, she moped around the condo.

On Tuesday Dave asked, "What the hell is going on with you? When I got home from my trip last week, you were so happy. Last night you behaved like somebody died."

He had hit her behavior on the head, she realized, wishing he weren't so perceptive. "I think I did something really stupid," she admitted.

"Sit down," he urged, and she curled up into a miserable ball on the leather couch. "Talk."

She told him what she and Maggie had done Wednesday. "It was wonderful." She was sure the pain showed.

He took her hand and spoke softly. "Don't look so stricken, sweetie. This too will pass." He smiled, taking some of the sting out of his next words. "You can't say I didn't warn you."

Searching his eyes, she found only sympathy. "I should have listened. I don't know what came over me."

"Lust." He lifted one eyebrow. "Give her time. She'll come around."

"Think so?" She clung to his words as if they were promises. "And you, Dave? What's going on with you?" Steve had vanished from their lives.

"Absolutely nothing. We can mourn together. Want a drink?"

"I don't think so."

* * * * *

At noon the next day, she waited in her office for a call from Maggie. It was Wednesday again, and she still hoped that Maggie would suggest going to dinner that night. At twelve forty-five she called Maggie's office. Maggie was out to lunch, the receptionist told her. Would she like to leave a message? "No," she said.

All week she had relived their lovemaking. She found she could not regret it, nor could she forget. Vividly remembered scenes appeared at odd moments, like today when she was talking to Phil Steir. She'd pictured herself cupping Maggie's breasts, speechless with wonder at what she was doing.

At five to one the phone rang. She forced herself to let it ring twice before snatching it to her ear. The disappointment left her feeling slightly ill. "Dave, what is it?"

"Just wondering how you were and if you're going to be home for dinner tonight. Thought I'd fix something special."

"Looks like I'll be home. I haven't heard from Maggie. But I've lost my appetite."

"I'm in a cooking mood. You just have to take a few bites and say a couple hallelujahs."

When they hung up, she heard the bell ring. The halls, reverberating with the sounds of children, became quiet as classroom doors closed. Lunch was over. So, apparently, were Wednesday night dinners with Maggie. She jumped when the phone pierced the quiet.

"I thought you weren't going to call." Suddenly weak, she leaned back in her chair.

"I went out to lunch," Maggie said. "Look, Erica, I think maybe it's best if we don't have dinner alone anymore."

"I was so afraid I'd never see you again," she went on as if she hadn't heard. "I'm sorry about last time."

A long pause. Then Maggie said, "Well, I'm as responsible as you are. I just don't think it should happen again."

Her hope hung on the word *think*. Maggie had not said she didn't *want* it to happen again. "It won't, Maggie."

"Let's cool it for a while. Okay?"

"Does that mean I won't see you tonight? I could bring Dave along." Would he go? He owed her.

Another silence. "See what he says. We could meet at Victoria's."

What he said was, "I'll cook for the two of you."

So, she called Maggie and told her. Maggie agreed to come over.

When Maggie stood outside the condo door, she wondered why she had accepted the invitation. She told herself she would leave if Dave left her alone with Erica. But when Erica opened the door and gave her a breathtaking smile, she remembered why she had succumbed to desire.

"Hey Maggie, how are you?" Dave said from the stove where he was sautéing onions and garlic in butter.

160

Did he know, she wondered. "Good, Dave. And you?" She agreed to a drink and leaned on the counter, sipping a vodka and tonic.

Erica was staring at her hungrily.

The intensity of the gaze disconcerted her. Feeling naked and more than a little vulnerable, she said, "Can I help?"

"You girls can make a salad."

"I saw Steve in the grocery store Saturday."

"It's all over. He's got a new boyfriend."

He had been with another man. That part she kept to herself. "Sorry."

"Don't be. It was an adventure." With a flourish he dropped shreds of pork into the frying pan. "Fried rice and egg drop soup."

She diced carrots, onions and green peppers, brushing elbows with Erica who was tearing up lettuce. She used her knife to scrape them off the cutting board onto the shredded greens. "Maybe that's how we should look at life."

"What? As fried rice and egg drop soup?" Dave said, grinning.

She laughed. "As an adventure. Then there would be no mistakes, no guilt."

"I don't believe in guilt," Dave remarked, adding rice to the sizzling mixture in the fry pan.

"Really?" she asked, once more leaning on the counter.

"Naw. The unconscious makes most of our decisions. That's why we often don't know the reasons for what we do."

"Where did you get that theory?" she asked him.

"It reminds me of something my therapist once said, that an affair is often used as a catalyst to make changes in a relationship."

"Think about something that you did that you don't understand. If you're honest with yourself, you'll find a hidden motive in your actions. Did you cheat on your husband when you wanted out of the marriage? Was he unfaithful?"

"Dave," Erica said, a protest.

Maggie appeared unfazed. She nodded. "Yes, and I never had before."

He shrugged. "You said yourself it's a common way to get out of a relationship. So, why should I try to keep Steve. Not only is it dangerous in our situation, but he doesn't want to be kept."

"So easy?" Erica asked.

His mouth twisted as he turned to smile at them both. "No, not easy at all."

"It's scary to think we're not in conscious control of what we do," Maggie remarked. It made her wonder. Maybe she had punished herself by tempting fate and grabbing too late for the bicycle light.

"Isn't it?" Dave wiped his hands on a towel. "Ready to eat?"

Later when they were alone, Erica asked Dave, "When did you get to be such a sage?"

"Did any of that make sense to you?" He stood up and stretched, his sweats gapping to reveal a flat, hairy belly.

"It made me think. Why have I never married?

God knows, I've had enough offers. But then I wondered if you said those things to make Maggie feel better about what she and I did."

"How would that make her feel better?" He stared down at her where she was sitting on the couch.

She ran her fingers through her hair. "That bit about not feeling guilty, implying that we're not consciously responsible for what we do."

"I said we don't always know the reasons." He yawned. "What do I know anyway? Most of it's just stuff I read or learned in counseling, just like she did."

"Thanks, Dave."

He gave her a crooked smile. "For being your personal buffer?"

"For fixing dinner, for making this evening possible."

Maggie had wanted to continue the conversation about the unconscious. It pained her to think that if Jo was carrying on with Gail, she was probably looking to end their commitment. Was their relationship so unsatisfying? But then she, herself, had also cheated. What were her reasons? To get even? Or had she used Jo's suspected infidelity to justify acting on her physical attraction toward Erica? Dave had said he didn't believe in guilt, that guilt was wasted energy and served no purpose. How nice it would be to think that way.

Light shone from the gap under Mike's bedroom

door. She opened her bedroom door and found Jo reading in bed. "No basketball on TV tonight?" she asked.

Looking up from her book, Jo said, "Get in here, darling. I need your body heat."

"Been home long?" She quickly undressed and climbed under the covers.

"Not so long. Where'd you have dinner?"

"Dave cooked for us. He's always good company. We talked about the unconscious."

Jo put her arm around her and drew her close. "Care to elaborate?"

"Oh, just stuff about how our lives are often orchestrated by hidden reasons."

"That so? Do you go along with that?"

"Some of it. Don't you sometimes do things you don't understand, that you think are out of character?"

Jo kissed her hair. "I suppose."

XVIII

March arrived, ushered in on warm breezes and cloudy skies. Rain fell on melting snow, causing minor flooding. Even before the rain stopped, Maggie and Jo, along with many others, responded to the promise of spring by going outside.

They took Bruno around several blocks, joining those walking, jogging and biking. Clouds raced overhead, spattering them with occasional showers. When the sun peeked out, they basked in its new-found warmth.

"How's your talk coming?" Maggie asked, referring to the upcoming assembly at Mike's high school.

"I'm pretty much ready. It's the sort of speech I give to other groups. I just tailor it toward the younger set." Jo looked skyward as they were briefly pelted by warm drops.

"I wish I could come. I've never heard you talk." She waited with Jo for Bruno to stop sniffing at a silver maple. "*Leisure* is doing an article about the Y. I told the photographer that he could film you and Gail playing racquetball on Wednesday night. That okay?"

She smiled. "Sure."

"Are you coming to Milwaukee with me this weekend?"

"I don't think so. I want to put the finishing touches on this talk and someone has to stay with Bruno and keep an eye on Mike. Or is he going?"

"No. He can take care of Bruno. Mike doesn't need a baby sitter anymore."

"You know what teenagers do when parents are away."

"I know, but we'll warn him. Come with me, Jo." They needed time away together. She recognized Jo's restlessness, even thought she understood it. She herself wanted a change.

Jo looked at her and smiled a little. "Going alone means you'll have prime time with Katherine and Shelley, a chance to talk without me getting in the way.

"You don't get in the way." They moved on to

another tree. Suddenly impatient, Maggie said, "Give him a jerk. We'll never get anywhere this way."

"What's the hurry?" But Jo tugged at the leash and they moved on at a brisk walk.

Maggie had plenty of time to think during the familiar drive to and from Milwaukee. Miles went by without her remembering any of the customary sights. She couldn't recall passing Fond du Lac at all going down, nor Oshkosh on the return trip. Jo's dissatisfaction occupied her mind. When she asked her what was wrong, Jo always said nothing.

She had been pleased to find Katherine and Paul apparently happy in their lives. Shelley had voiced some complaints about the university, but in general she appeared to be satisfactorily involved in her studies and her life as a coed. Shelley had shared some of her experiences with her, regaling her with campus stories, setting her mind at ease with her frankness.

As she neared the end of her drive home and the weekend, her thoughts turned to Erica. She had not been able to put their lovemaking to rest. By resolutely banishing it whenever it came to mind, she thought it would fade. But just when she thought she'd succeeded, she would suddenly picture them together on the leather couch or in Erica's bed as if it had happened yesterday.

They still met for Wednesday night dinner either

at a restaurant or with Dave at the condo, never alone. There was an almost magnetic attraction between them whenever they were together. When Jo was around, she and Erica put on a show of casual friendship.

She had not talked to Jo over the weekend and wondered what she'd missed by being gone. Happy to see the van in the driveway, she parked in the garage and went looking for Jo.

Bruno tore around the side of the house to greet her. Covered with mud, he shook vigorously while wagging his tail and showing his teeth in a small grin of welcome.

"Hi, pooch. Been rolling in mud puddles, I see. Don't you dare jump on me." She held his affection at arm's length as she walked to the back yard where Jo and Mike were raking sodden leaves.

"Look who's here." Jo dropped her rake.

"Hey, Mom, you're just in time. We're almost done."

"Hi. Everyone says hello." She watched Bruno flop down in a low, wet spot. "That's one filthy dog."

"I'll wash him with the hose," Mike promised.

Removing her dirty tennies and work gloves, Jo followed her inside to the bedroom. "I missed you."

"You should have come with me." She grabbed Jo and covered her face and neck with passionate kisses.

Jo laughed. "Does this mean you missed me too?" And as they hugged, "You're going to get dirty."

"All right, then. That's enough." She backed away and looked at her clothes. "Anything exciting happen while I was gone?"

"Well, Nancy and Liz came over for dinner last night. We had sort of a potluck. We went to the sports show out at the mall. Saw Gail and Erica there. I almost bought a boat. I didn't want to do it without you."

She looked into Jo's smiling, gray eyes. Her freckles had darkened a little, no longer winter pale. "What kind of boat?"

"A bass boat, of course. What else?" Jo grinned, showing straight, white teeth.

She said, "You know how much I love fishing."

"I know. You'd rather put me on a hook." Jo got up and looked out the window. "If Mike weren't out there, I'd take you to bed right now."

"Later," she promised.

Erica had spent the weekend with Gail. She didn't know what to do about her feelings toward Maggie, except to divert them with other pursuits. Gail behaved listlessly, seeming almost wounded. When she asked her if something was wrong, Gail shook her head.

"Nothing you can fix, my friend."

She assumed that what she couldn't fix had to do with Jo. "Well, let's just have a good time then."

"Sounds like a plan," Gail had agreed.

Sunday afternoon they went to a movie and out to eat with Dave, who had been in a funereal mood for days. "We shouldn't have gone to see *Philadelphia*," Dave remarked when they were seated at the restaurant. "All I need to top my mood off right now is to find a cockroach in my dinner, dead or alive."

"Yech." Gail crinkled her nose. "I forgot. That

happened here, didn't it, months ago? They promised to clean up the kitchen."

"Actually, every restaurant has roaches," Dave said. "They just don't admit it. They usually bring in the exterminators regularly."

"I suggested seeing something else," Erica reminded him. She was becoming impatient with the funk that hung over everyone like a black cloud.

"Yeah, like *Schindler's List*. That's a real upper too. At least when you see that, you're not thinking there but for the grace of God, go I." Dave looked around the room.

She said, "It could have been you had you been alive and in Europe. You'd have worn a pink triangle in Hitler's Germany."

"That's a lot of ifs," Gail pointed out.

The waiter brought their drinks to the table and took their food orders. Each requested a different entree, Dave's suggestion. That way they could sample each other's dinners, he said.

"What's on for this week?" he asked.

"Tuesday afternoon we principals congregate at the high school for an assembly on substance and alcohol abuse and depression. Jo's one of the speakers. Should be interesting, if not cheery." She watched Gail while she said this. Gail's gaze remained on her drink.

"Most of the kids around here are into alcohol, not drugs. Right?" Dave asked.

She nodded. "Even kids in grade school drink." She thought of Carl Jablonski, who had been suspended last week for consuming beer on school grounds. He might not even make it to junior high.

Except this time, his father recognized a problem and threatened to beat him. A lot of good that would do, she mused.

"Even around here we get babies born with alcohol addiction. Those kids never have much of a chance in life. Short attention spans, damaged nervous systems." Gail paused. "How the hell did we get on this subject? Let's liven up the conversation."

"Did I ever tell you about my first sexual experience?" Dave asked.

He had recently told Erica, but she laughed as he repeated the story to Gail. He had been a bumbling novice, trying to fool a man of experience.

"After I slipped and impaled myself on the bed, he asked me if this was my first time. I admitted I'd had countless encounters with women, but had never been with a man before him. He looked at the ceiling and asked how he had gotten so unlucky. He suggested that I stick with the women and leave the men alone to poke each other in the right places. I should have bit his cock off, but he wouldn't let me near it anymore."

When they reached home, she asked him if the story was true.

"No. It was much more humiliating than that. I was a classic case of pre-ejaculation. Before I even got my underwear off, I came. He was furious with me."

Arriving with Phil Steir at LaFollette High at twelve-thirty on Tuesday, Erica took a front row seat in the auditorium. She waved at Jo, who was on stage with the high school principal, vice principal, superintendent and the other speaker.

As she chatted with Phil, the auditorium slowly filled with students and teachers and administrators.

She turned as Jo waved at Mike, who was taking a seat in the forward section, and smiled as he gave them each a brief, embarrassed salute.

At one the principal welcomed those in the audience and introduced the people onstage. Jo would be the first to speak. She walked to the podium.

Erica had never seen Jo dressed in a suit, much less doing her job. She was impressed by her professionalism. Addressing the audience, she seemed at ease and sure of herself.

Jo glanced at her notes, looked up and stopped talking. She appeared puzzled and frowned a little. Erica turned to follow her gaze as a ripple of alarm buzzed through the audience.

A skinny man brandishing something was running down the center aisle. He was shouting, but at first she couldn't understand the words. Then she recognized him. Jon Hunter. Adrenaline shot through her like an electric shock and her heart bumped into overtime.

As he came closer, she heard him hollering, "Where are you? Fucking cunts."

She saw the small revolver in his hand as he neared the stage. Phil started to rise from his seat next to her. She was half out of her chair. The babble of voices increased in volume.

A woman maybe twenty rows back stood up, made her way to the center aisle, and dashed toward the rear double doors.

Shots reverberated through the auditorium, and Erica jerked as if hit herself. She thought the woman went down but she couldn't be sure, because people along the aisle were standing now. It seemed like everyone was yelling.

Hunter jumped on the stage and scuttled along the edge. He paused in front of her. They stared at each other. "You," he said accusingly.

Her heart leaped into her throat, making it difficult to breathe. "Jon," she said as Phil launched himself toward the stage. She heard the shot after the bullet slammed into her shoulder, forcing her back into her seat. Only then did she know she was hit. By that time he was gone.

The auditorium went quiet for a brief moment, then erupted into sound and motion. Screaming, shouting people jumped seats and pushed past her toward aisles and exits. She observed the crowd with detached interest even as the right side of her chest burgeoned into a red blossom.

They were calling her name. She looked at Phil and Jo, who leaned over her. Behind Jo was Mike — their faces pale, their pupils huge.

"I called for an ambulance and the police are on their way," someone said. "Should we move her?"

"Let's put her on the stage." Phil lifted her in his arms.

Her chest burned as he took hold of her, but she gave him a smile anyway.

"Better put something on that," Jo said.

Phil tore off his shirt and placed it under her suit jacket.

"You'll ruin it," Erica said. Her breath came in short pants, because it hurt to breathe at all. There were still people rushing past, some stopping to stare. She had a sense of being in the center of a storm, buffeted by swirling winds. "Hunter? The woman?"

"Don't talk," Phil said. "The ambulance will be here soon."

The emergency medical technicians arrived shortly after. They checked the wound, covered it, inserted a needle in her hand for intravenous fluids and loaded her onto a gurney.

"Mrs. Hunter's dead," someone said as the EMTs wheeled her toward the nearest exit.

The woman who ran down the aisle, she realized. Then wondered if this was how Maggie had felt when she broke her neck. Sort of distant, as if she were standing on the sidelines watching the action. Perhaps that's what made it bearable.

XIX

"Jo called," the receptionist told Maggie when she returned from the restroom. "She said not to alarm you, that she and Mike are all right, but something happened at the high school during her talk. You're to go to Theda Clark as soon as you can."

What could possibly have gone wrong, she wondered, turning on the car radio and tuning into a local station. Only music accompanied her swift drive to the hospital. She pulled into the parking lot across from emergency and hurried inside. An unpleasant sense of déjà vu pervaded the place. She realized she had spent enough time here with her broken neck to last her a lifetime.

Immediately spotting Jo and Mike, she walked over to where they sat. Mike was paging through a magazine. Jo stared into space. She thought they appeared strangely distraught. They looked startled when she said, "Hi. What happened? Why are you here?"

Mike blurted, "This crazy guy killed Mrs. Hunter and shot Erica."

"No," she said with disbelief, looking at Jo for confirmation. Her legs turned weak, and without waiting for Jo to speak she went to the desk to ask about Erica.

The receptionist said she would check again on Erica's condition.

She turned to Jo who had followed her. "Did you get hold of Dave?"

Sounding aggrieved, Jo said, "I already asked about Erica. A nurse should be letting us know soon." Then she added, "I don't know where Dave works. I called the condo and left a message."

At Erica's request, Maggie and Jo were allowed into the emergency room. "Strange how the worm turns, isn't it?" Erica said, her smile wan, her face waxen. "I'd be going home, I think, if I hadn't lost a lot of blood."

They could see that her shoulder and chest were wrapped under the hospital gown. The bullet had passed clean through the soft part between arm and shoulder without damaging any bones. A clear solution in a plastic bag dripped toward her hand.

"Did they give you a transfusion?" Jo asked.

"I refused one. Because of that and possible infection, I might be here a few days." Her voice sounded thin.

She would have said no to a stranger's blood too, Maggie thought — just to be safe. "You can stay with us when you get out," she offered, feeling Jo's glance.

"Thanks, but I'll be all right at home."

"Where does Dave work?" Jo asked.

"He could be out visiting doctors. Who knows. Maybe he's even here," Erica said.

Maggie gave Mike a key to the Grand Am, so he could go home. Then she and Jo followed Erica as she was pushed through the halls to her room. None of this seemed real to her yet.

Jo whispered, "I wonder if Mike is really all right. It was a violent afternoon. And it all happened in less than twenty minutes."

"I don't know," she replied. "He said he was."

Erica remained hospitalized three days, until her blood count began to multiply and her vital signs stabilized. Her mother flew in from Arizona, even though she had told her she was not in any danger.

"I had to see for myself that you're all right," her mother said when she arrived. "And now I can meet your friends."

Plagued by nightmares of Hunter chasing her with intent to kill, she feared sleep. Yet she had trouble staying awake and even more difficulty awakening from the clutches of these dreams.

Having her mother take care of her comforted her

more than she had imagined — although she knew whatever she herself couldn't do alone, Dave or Maggie or Jo or Gail would do for her.

One week after the shooting, her shoulder throbbed and itched mercilessly. They'd eaten dinner Saturday night at Maggie's and Jo's. Liz and Nancy had been there. Sunday Maggie and Jo and Gail had come to the condo for a feast prepared by Dave with her mother's assistance.

"You have wonderful friends, darling. They're very supportive," her mother said, setting up two TV trays in the living room Monday noon. "You're not sleeping with Dave, are you?"

"It's hard to discuss that stuff with you, Mom," she protested. Her mother had just fixed lunch. "You're going to make me fat."

"You don't have an extra ounce on you, Erica, and you know it."

"I should go back to work next week."

"Don't push yourself, dear." Her mother sat on the couch next to her.

"Are you having a good time, Mom? You can stay on, you know." She and her mother played endless games of Spite and Malice, alternating them with Scrabble.

"I'm enjoying myself. But I miss the warmth. When you go back to work, I think I'll go home."

"I don't want you to leave." Her mother was a safe haven. It had been like returning to the nest.

Her mother patted her on the knee. "You come and visit and bring your friends with you. You're especially fond of Maggie, aren't you?"

Was she so transparent? Probably not to anyone else. "How about a game of Scrabble?"

When she and Dave saw her mother to the plane Sunday, she cried. Her right arm hung in a sling to take pressure off the wounded musculature.

"We're always saying goodbye, aren't we?" her mother said, blinking away tears. "I could stay a little longer."

"I won't be home, Mom. What would you do all day?"

"If you find you can't work, come stay with me. I'm sure the school will give you leave." Her mother kissed and carefully hugged her.

" 'Bye, Louise. Come whenever you can," Dave said, giving her mother a hug before she went out the gate to the waiting plane.

She and Dave stood by the windows until the jet taxied to the runway and took off, airborne for Chicago.

"I'd put my arm around you, sweetie, but I don't want to hurt you," he said.

"It's okay, Dave. I'm just a little more emotional than usual. I always cry when I leave my mother or she leaves me."

"You're really going back to work tomorrow?"

"I have to or I might never go back." She sniffed and fished in her pocket for a tissue. "I've got school phobia."

* * * * *

Three weeks had passed since the shootings at LaFollette High. Erica was back at work. Mike walked around looking as if he never slept. Jo said she was experiencing difficulties dealing with what had happened to Mrs. Hunter and Erica. She'd referred all counseling resulting from the shootings to others in the office.

Then, on a Saturday morning, she told Maggie she was going to stay with Liz and Nancy for a while. They were in the bedroom, the only room where they were assured of privacy.

"Why?" Maggie asked, dumbfounded.

Jo shrugged. "I need time away."

"Away from me?" The question hurt.

"I think I asked you to move in before I resolved my feelings for Gail."

"I knew Gail was at the bottom of this." They were still in bed, talking about separation during the time they usually made love. "It's your house. Mike and I'll move out."

"No," Jo said flatly. "I don't want you to move."

"You're doing this so that you can see Gail, aren't you?" She sat up and crossed her arms.

"I'm the problem, not Gail." Jo lay on her back, her hands under her head, her gray eyes dark with trouble.

"You're thinking that life is too short, and you want to be able to do whatever you want. It's got to do with the shootings, doesn't it?" She studied Jo's prone form. "But, Jo, if you leave me, you're also freeing me." She could do anything with Erica then.

Jo tilted her head toward Maggie. "Is that a threat?"

Her chest tightened painfully. She felt vaguely

nauseated. So much for ignoring Jo's liaison with Gail, hoping it would die of its own accord. She was being abandoned by her supposed best friend, the one person she should be able to trust above all others. Unexpected tears surprised her.

"Don't," Jo whispered, drawing her down into her arms and kissing the salty wetness.

She shook with sobs, even as Jo's caresses slowly became demanding. Unexpectedly aroused, she responded.

Yet as they moved toward climax, stroking each other intimately, kissing fiercely, she knew it would change nothing. Consumed by lust, she tasted the passion they created and cried out when desire burst into orgasm.

The next day Jo packed a few bags. Liz and Nancy had been over the night before, trying to change Jo's mind and assuring Maggie that they weren't taking sides.

Maggie was there when Jo told Mike in the morning that she was leaving.

"Where you going?" he asked.

She told him, and he stared at her in disbelief. However, true to character, he said nothing more.

He had finally accepted her, Maggie realized, and she was inexplicably moving out. Watching him retreat to his room, she knew he was writing Jo off as unreliable.

After that, Jo hurried to get out of the house. Maggie knew she was not making it easy for her as she silently watched her pack.

"I'll call tonight or tomorrow," Jo said as she went out to the garage.

The house was silent once Jo was gone. Maggie knocked on Mike's door.

"What?" he said impatiently.

"You want to talk?" Silly question to ask someone who was so reticent.

"No." The door remained closed.

"I'm taking Bruno for a walk. Want to come with us?" Bruno stood attentively by her side, his tail wagging, his eyes hopeful. She was sure he recognized the word "walk."

"No, thanks."

"Okay," she said to the dog, whose whole body was wagging now. "Let's find your leash."

He nearly knocked her down getting to the door.

They walked for hours. Bruno must have thought his pads were going to fall off. When they both finally started to drag, she took him home to the quiet house.

Mike had left a note: *Gone with TJ.*

Calling Erica Monday at noon, she wondered how to say that Jo had left. She felt as if she'd been in shock all weekend. It had happened so quickly, the telling and the leaving.

"Liz and Nancy told me yesterday," Erica said. "I'm sorry, Maggie."

"We can eat out any night we want to now," Maggie remarked. The humiliation of rejection had finally hit home, and she smarted under it.

"Do you want to go out tonight?" Erica asked,

then remembered she had a meeting with the school board at seven.

"I can't, anyway. Mike's been a worry ever since that disastrous assembly. It's too soon to tell how he feels about Jo walking out, but he spent most of yesterday in his room." It seemed like everyone had gone crazy in the wake of the shootings. "Do you know any good counselors?"

"Why don't you get him into the crisis center. They were on the scene at school afterwards, weren't they?"

"Thanks. I'll give them a call. How are you doing?" After all, Erica had suffered more damage than anyone other than Mrs. Hunter.

"I'm alive and grateful for it. Although I have to admit I'm a little paranoid."

"Do you still have nightmares?"

"Those too."

Maggie made the effort not to sound bitter. "I'm still digesting all of this." She felt as if she was being punished for Hunter's actions. He had been charged with first degree murder, while the damaging repercussions of his crime rippled in ever widening circles.

"The afternoon of the shooting is a blur to me. Some days I have to touch my arm to know it happened. Denial, maybe."

"When are you getting the sling off?"

"Three weeks. The itching is driving me crazy."

"Let's go out Wednesday night. I'll go nuts if I don't get away."

When she hung up, she called the county crisis center. The phone worker put her through to a male counselor, and she told him the circumstances. He agreed to see Mike the next afternoon. She'd have to leave work early to get him there by four p.m.

Her life had flip-flopped. She coped as she had when she'd broken her neck, managing the days moment by moment.

XX

May gave some balance to winter's hardships, Erica thought as she drove home from work with her car windows open. She couldn't soak up enough sun and presented an eager face to the warm air. Appreciatively sniffing the new growth, she gazed with wonder at the translucent leaves and flowering growth.

Changing clothes quickly, she left a note for Dave and climbed behind the wheel of the Cutlass again. She no longer wore the sling, but her shoulder was stiff and she underwent physical therapy once a week in hopes of limbering it up. She doubted if she'd be playing tennis this summer. If so, she'd have to draft Dave to play with her. She seldom saw Gail or Jo.

She parked at the top of the hill at High Cliff and spotted Maggie leaning against the side of her Grand Am. Locking the car doors, she walked over to her. "Great day, isn't it?"

"Marvelous." Maggie nodded, smiling. She brushed dark strands away from her face, which had been brightened by the elements, and faced the warm wind. "How are you?"

Wondering at the strong feelings Maggie always generated in her, she murmured, "I'm crazy about you."

Maggie turned back, shadows on her face. "What?"

"Nothing. I'm fine. Something wrong?" Jo again, she supposed.

"Let's not spoil the evening." Maggie walked quickly toward the path that led along the edge of the bluffs. From this northeast corner they could see as much of Lake Winnebago as the eye could take in, certainly not all of its thirty-mile length or twelve-mile width. White wakes trailed boats the size of toys. Tree-tops swayed far below them. The path they took made its way through woods. Rocky precipices that had eroded away from the cliff walls jutted into space, islands in the air.

She took long steps to keep up with Maggie's agitated stride. What was going on? Maggie's behavior put off questions. She ventured a statement. "You must have talked to Jo."

"You can tell?"

"It always puts you in a mood."

"I told her I was looking for another place. She doesn't want me to leave the house. She asked me to wait a few more weeks."

"For what?" She walked close to Maggie, listening with worry.

"For her to make up her mind, I guess, about whether she wants to live with me."

"This is insane, Maggie."

Maggie glanced at her. "Maybe not. It gives us all a breather. If you're going to be with someone, you shouldn't divide yourself with someone else. And that's what we were all doing. I think the Jon Hunter thing just blew us out of the water."

"I want you to be with me," she heard herself say, then held her breath.

Maggie gave her a small smile, maybe to soften her words. "I'm not going to be with anyone else until it's all over with Jo. I don't want to be responsible for anybody's pain but my own ever again." She had left Bill, nearly lost her kids with her behavior, cheated on Jo.

"I love you, Maggie." There, she had said it. Her heart thumped with alarm.

Maggie put an arm around her and squeezed. She smiled warmly, her eyes flashing emotion. "I know you do, Erica. I love you too."

She took hope. "Then why can't we try?" She put a hand on Maggie's shoulder.

"I just told you why. Please, let's just let it go for now."

Shrugging off sadness, Erica replied, "Okay. Have it your way."

"Thanks." Maggie gave her another hug and let her arm drop to her side. "Think they'll put Hunter in the loony bin?"

"Yep. He'll never pay for murdering his wife. Poor woman. Guess the key is not to get involved with someone like that in the first place."

They stood on a promontory, overlooking the huge lake. Neither spoke for a few moments. The water far below them stretched as far south as they could see. The north shore was dotted with homes. Across the expanse of waves, the water towers of Neenah-Menasha rose above the cities. The sun cast long streaks of light from behind a bank of clouds.

"Are you hungry yet?" she asked. They were planning dinner at the nearby supper club.

"Starved. How about you?" Maggie squinted at the bright rays.

"We better start back."

Over dinner, she asked, "Are you coming home with me?" Maggie had spent many evenings at the condo, dating back to Jo's moving out.

"For a while," Maggie answered. She had yet to leave Mike overnight, not knowing how to explain her absence to him.

Erica visibly relaxed. Her appetite for Maggie was insatiable. It was like she'd been starved all these years and couldn't get enough sex. She worried about what she would do if Jo came back into the picture.

The position of high school principal was available at Point. Erica stared at the bulletin on her desk.

She didn't really want to move away from the Fox Cities, but this was a rare opportunity. She'd have to put together an updated resumé and a letter asking for an interview. Point was a nice place to live, ecology minded, centered close to parks, lakes, and forests along the Wisconsin River.

Applying for the job didn't mean she had to take it. If her relationship with Maggie showed some promise of becoming permanent, she wouldn't consider leaving. But if Jo came back into Maggie's life, moving away might be an option she wanted to pursue. When she went home that evening, she remembered to take the job bulletin with her.

"You're looking at this position in Point?" Dave asked, staring at the notice as he stood at the kitchen table.

"Well, I thought I should interview anyway. I probably won't get it." She was filling water glasses for dinner.

He postured disbelief. "You'd have to move away. What about you and Maggie? What about me?"

She laughed. "You should have been an actor, Dave. It's a good opportunity. I have to think about my career. And what if Jo and Maggie get back together?"

"Don't I count?" He frowned at her.

His obvious indignation amused her. "Of course, you do. But it'll give you incentive to get on with your life. And me too. Besides, this is stupid. I haven't even applied, much less landed an interview."

"Wait till you taste this dinner." He extracted a casserole from the oven. "You'll never leave me."

"I certainly will miss you if I do leave. When we

retire and no longer need sex, we can grow old together." She put placemats on the table and dishes and tableware.

"Think that's going to happen? The bit about sex?"

"Not at the rate I'm going. I never enjoyed sex like I do now."

"Not even when you had me?" He grinned boyishly at her while she fumbled with an explanation. "I understand, sweetie. You found yourself the right partner. Hang onto her."

"If I only could," she said, sitting down. "I'm sorry, Dave. I wasn't thinking. I enjoyed doing it with you."

"And I with you. But it wasn't meant to be. Right?" He set the casserole on the table, along with freshly baked bread and a salad. "Eat."

She heaped food on her plate and took a bite. "Mmm. Good. You cook better than you make love anyway."

He sat down. "That's not a compliment, Erica. Men are very serious about their sexual prowess, and I'm no exception."

"Maggie? I'm sorry. I dialed the wrong number," Jo said.

"Meant to get Gail, did you?" Maggie said acidly. "Never mind, Jo. I need to talk to you anyway. There are bats in the attic. They keep escaping into the house." Last night she and Mike had chased them around with a landing net. During her weekend visit, Shelley had been awakened by one swooping

190

overhead. "We get them out by chasing them through open doors at night, but I think they come right back in."

"I'll call a pest control company, but I don't think they're allowed to exterminate bats."

"Well, maybe they can find where they're getting in and plug the hole during the night. Of course, the babies will be left behind." An unfortunate result. "How are you, Jo?"

"All right. And you and Mike?"

"Mike's doing well in track, especially the hurdles. I thought he'd break his legs, but he's breaking records instead."

"Congratulate him for me. I'll come over tomorrow evening and look for the bat hole myself."

"Mike searched for the opening over the weekend, after one woke Shelley in the night." She had run screaming from the furry, chattering creature. "The bat was probably as terrified as she was."

Jo laughed. "Sorry. Will you be home?"

"Yes, as a matter of fact." No track meets, no other commitments.

When they hung up, the phone rang almost immediately, and Harriet Paynter identified herself.

"Maggie, are you and Jo coming to the lake Memorial Day weekend?" For years they had spent that weekend at Paynters' Resort. "We got your Christmas card and note. I was delighted to hear that you recovered so well."

Since Jo left, she hadn't thought beyond one weekend ahead as to what she wanted to do. "I'm sorry. I hope you didn't hold a cottage for us."

"You can stay in our home, if you'll come watch over the resort. We're supposed to go to North

Carolina for the weekend." They had a son living there, along with his wife and children. "I probably should have called earlier, but you know how time gets away. Especially when you're busy."

She liked Harriet and Donald, and she missed the lake. Who would pass up an opportunity to stay on the water for nothing? "I'd love to come. I don't think Jo will be able to make it, but maybe my son and daughter will join me along with a friend. Would that be okay?"

"Wonderful. Mike and Shelley? I haven't seen them in a couple summers."

"You would have seen them last year if I hadn't broken my neck and cut short the vacation." Already she was planning the few days. What to take for food, for clothes. "How are you and Don?"

"Great. The fish are biting and Don has time to outwit a few every evening. So he's in seventh heaven. The lake is beautiful and I have a couple hours a day to read. It's the best time of year for us. But we're gearing up for summer. Putting in the pier, repairing winter damage."

"When do you want me there?"

"Can you come Friday morning. Our plane leaves at noon. We'll be back late Monday night. You don't have to wait. And if we're gone when you get here, the key will be in the bell on the porch. I'll write down everything you need to know, including our Donny's phone number, and leave it on the kitchen counter."

She could take off work Friday, she supposed. Everybody slacked off the day before a holiday weekend anyway.

XXI

The next evening when Jo arrived, Maggie had already debated whether to tell her about Harriet Paynter's phone call and decided to say nothing.

The sight of the van in the driveway brought back comfortably familiar feelings. Jo could have been coming home from work as she had so many nights in the past. But then the anger followed, overriding everything else, and an edge crept into her voice when she said hello.

Jo slammed the door of the Caravan and turned

to smile. "Bats in the belfry, lady?" She raised her eyebrows.

Smiling faintly at the pun, Maggie leaned on the side of the van. She wanted to be free of the emotions Jo set into motion. Standing in the driveway with the late afternoon sun warming her, she wondered if it was ever possible to regain damaged trust, to heal wounded feelings. She squinted at Jo, who looked no different yet was disconcertingly unfamiliar. "I'll help you get the ladder."

"You can hold it for me."

They circled the outside of the house with no success. The entryway for the bats could easily be overlooked, since the flying mammals would be able to squeeze through a tiny space.

Jo clambered down. "I'll just have to call the pest control people. I don't see anything that resembles a bat door. I hope they don't bother you anymore before they can get here."

Mike hadn't returned home. She had told him Jo was coming today, and she wondered if he was avoiding her. "We were careless. The attic door was cracked open. It's shut tight now. So maybe they won't be able to get downstairs. Want to come in?"

"I can't. I'll just put the ladder away."

She wouldn't ask again. "Okay, Jo. See you around. I should tell you, though, that I'm still looking at apartments."

"Can't you just give me a little time?" Jo hung the ladder in the garage.

"How much time, Jo? And why should I put my life on hold?"

"I thought you were doing pretty much what you wanted to do." Jo looked away. "Was Erica tested after she and Dave broke up?"

"I'll tell her you asked." She went inside and slammed the door. Closing her eyes, she gritted her teeth. It was amazing, she thought, how Jo managed to disillusion her.

"Maggie." Jo knocked on the door and tried it. "I'm sorry. I don't want anything to happen to you. Please let me in."

She shot the deadbolt in place. "Go away. Leave me alone."

Erica drove to Paynter's Resort from Point the Friday afternoon of Memorial Day weekend. Deep in thought, she found herself in Wild Rose having completely missed her turn and was forced to backtrack. She thought the interview had gone well. The superintendent and board members had hinted that she was a serious contender. She would be called back for a second interview in a week or two.

Bouncing down the sandy driveway, she felt the excitement she always experienced before meeting Maggie — compounded this time by the sheer joy of spending a couple days in a lovely spot on the water.

She parked behind the house and walked down the steps next to it that led to the sandy beach. A pair of blue jays screeched from the pine trees beside her. Maggie sat in a webbed chaise longue near the shoreline. Gulls screamed over the lake. Water lapped at the shore. Reeds poked here and there out of the stretch of sand. The sky overhead was a blue dome from which the sun radiated heat.

Bruno, who was rushing back and forth in the shallow water biting at waves, splashed out of the lake and ran toward her.

Maggie turned and grinned. She stood up, setting her book down. "So, you found it."

"After a few wrong turns. Not because of poor directions, though."

Maggie led her back up the steps to the open porch overlooking the lake. "Let's sit here. Can I get you anything?"

"Not right now." She sat down and smiled at Maggie. "Have I really known you less than a year? It doesn't seem possible."

"It's been an eventful year. Why were you in Point?"

She told her about the interview. "I didn't say anything earlier, because there was really nothing to say."

"You'd have to move," Maggie pointed out. "I'd miss you terribly."

"I wouldn't even think of moving if there was a chance you and I might be together," she murmured, watching Bruno in the water.

"I wish this were happening next year, not now."

"Me too." A sad, lonely sensation washed over her. She wanted Maggie to tell her not to take the position. That would give her the thread of hope she needed. "Well, I don't have the job and I may not get it."

* * * * *

Saturday morning unveiled a day as warm as the end of June, not May. Maggie remembered countless rainy, cold, windy Memorial Day weekends. The breeze, drifting through the open windows, was summer-warm and laden with the odors of lake and pines.

Shifting her body toward Erica, who lay sleeping beside her, she suddenly realized that the pain at the base of her skull was gone. She couldn't have said when it went away. The strain of turning sometimes made her neck ache, but the constant throb had left her. Getting up quietly, she let herself out on the deck.

With a start, she recognized Jo standing with shoes in hand in the shallows. She shook her head as if to clear a vision. Crossing her arms, she hugged the terrycloth robe to herself. At a loss as to what to do, she turned away. Sliding open the heavy glass door, she ducked indoors.

Erica opened her eyes. Even heavy-lidded and rumpled with sleep, she looked gorgeous. Holding out her arms, she said, "Come back to bed."

"Later," she promised.

"Your kids are coming later. I want you."

"Jo's out there."

But when they searched for signs of Jo, there were none. No van, no footprints. It gave Maggie an eerie feeling as if she'd imagined seeing Jo.

"Okay, let's go back to bed," she said, knowing that any carefree desire had flown out the window.

* * * * *

Erica left Monday afternoon. "Love you, Maggie," she said as she honked the horn and drove away.

Having fought the urge to cry since Saturday morning, it was a relief to let the tears roll down her face. She couldn't remember a more bittersweet weekend. Would the joy of loving Maggie be worth the pain of losing her? Was it Shakespeare who wrote it was better to have loved and lost than not to have loved at all? Had it been in the form of a question? She didn't recall.

If the job at Point was offered to her, she knew now that she would take it. Point wasn't so far from the Fox Cities. She would see Maggie. Perhaps they would even become a couple, but it wasn't going to happen soon.

She told herself she'd better stop crying or she'd have an accident, and then wondered if that would be so bad. Maybe it would free her of this crushing sadness that otherwise only time would take care of.

Mike, who now possessed a temporary driving permit, drove Maggie home late Monday afternoon. His friend, T.J., had taken him to the lake Saturday. Bruno, smelling of the water in which he'd spent most of the weekend, panted from the back seat.

Pleasantly tired from sun and wind and swimming, she said, "Everybody needs a few days away now and then, don't you think?"

Mike grunted.

"Your dad'll be home soon, Mike. Have you thought about where you want to live?"

"I like it here. I don't want to go back to Milwaukee."

Inordinately pleased, she said, "I like you here too."

When they turned into the driveway, Jo's van was parked in its usual space. Mike braked next to it. He got out of the Grand Am, released the dog and opened the trunk. She sat in the car collecting her thoughts. She didn't want a fight in front of Mike. It might change his mind about staying.

After carrying in the suitcases and cooler, Mike made a phone call. "T.J.'s picking me up, Mom."

"Tonight?" she asked stupidly. She was putting away the food. Jo was nowhere in sight.

"In a few minutes." He put a large hand on her shoulder, surprising her with an affectionate squeeze. "Got to change clothes."

When he left with T.J., she began searching for Jo. She was startled to see Jo's clothes back in the closets. Thinking to look in the park, she took Bruno with her. She found Jo sitting on a bench with her arms spread across the back. Bruno lunged toward her.

"Sit down," Jo said, moving over to make room. She took the dog's large head between her hands and scratched behind his ears. He whined softly. "Why didn't you tell me you were going to the lake?"

She sat sideways, so that she could look at Jo. "Why would I?"

Jo gave her a troubled glance. "It was our getaway. You shared it with Erica."

"So I did," she said, maintaining a flat tone. "You're moving back in. I haven't found an apartment yet."

"I asked you not to look." Jo reached for her hand. "Can we try to get past what's happened?"

The last of the light had left the sky, leaving the river lit only by reflections. Street lamps cast a soft glow over them. "What about Gail?"

"I haven't done right by Gail either. If she can't settle for friendship, I'll have to stop seeing her. Can you do the same with Erica?"

She met Jo's eyes. The gaze felt naked and filled with despair. She knew in that instant that Jo had not been able to let her go, had unwillingly made a choice. Well, it was true for her too, she thought. She had stayed on at the house, waiting for Jo to choose. Was that partly because her broken neck had left her in debt to Jo's many months of care? Whatever the reason, they had to either put an end to what was between them or move it to a new dimension.

"I can try." Already she missed Erica in bed, knowing that they might never love each other that way again.

"Do you find it strange, Maggie, that your broken neck brought out the best in us, while Jon Hunter's craziness exposed the worst?"

"I thought you were running scared. Grabbing for everything." She squeezed Jo's hand. "What we should have learned from my accident and maybe didn't was to enjoy every day, because you never know what's going to happen."

Jo bent to pat the dog, now lying at her feet. "Why aren't we ever satisfied, Maggie?"

"Don't always analyze everything, Jo. When my nose was to the pavement, all I wanted was to be able to move my arms and legs. Is that enough now? No, of course not. We'd still be sitting around fires exchanging grunts if we were easily satisfied."

Jo brightened. "You're right, sweetie. I think too much."

"That's not it, Jo. You think you have control over what happens in your life."

"I have control over me," Jo insisted. A gleam had appeared in her eyes. She was enjoying herself.

The conversation felt familiar and comfortable, like an old rerun. Maggie smiled a little. If they could just keep the dialogue going, they might have a chance. "Do you? Well, then we need to have a serious discussion over your behavior lately."

A few of the publications of
THE NAIAD PRESS, INC.
P.O. Box 10543 • Tallahassee, Florida 32302
Phone (904) 539-5965
Toll-Free Order Number: 1-800-533-1973
Mail orders welcome. Please include 15% postage.

CHANGES by Jackie Calhoun. 208 pp. Involved romance and relationships.　　　　ISBN 1-56280-083-3　$10.95

FAIR PLAY by Rose Beecham. 256 pp. 3rd Amanda Valentine Mystery.　　　　ISBN 1-56280-081-7　10.95

PAXTON COURT by Diane Salvatore. 256 pp. Erotic and wickedly funny contemporary tale about the business of learning to live together.　　　　ISBN 1-56280-109-0　21.95

PAYBACK by Celia Cohen. 176 pp. A gripping thriller of romance, revenge and betrayal.　　　　ISBN 1-56280-084-1　10.95

THE BEACH AFFAIR by Barbara Johnson. 224 pp. Sizzling summer romance/mystery/intrigue.　　　　ISBN 1-56280-090-6　10.95

GETTING THERE by Robbi Sommers. 192 pp. Nobody does it like Robbi!　　　　ISBN 1-56280-099-X　10.95

FINAL CUT by Lisa Haddock. 208 pp. 2nd Carmen Ramirez Mystery.　　　　ISBN 1-56280-088-4　10.95

FLASHPOINT by Katherine V. Forrest. 256 pp. A Lesbian blockbuster!　　　　ISBN 1-56280-079-5　10.95

DAUGHTERS OF A CORAL DAWN by Katherine V. Forrest. Audio Book — read by Jane Merrow.　　　ISBN 1-56280-110-4　16.95

CLAIRE OF THE MOON by Nicole Conn. Audio Book —Read by Marianne Hyatt.　　　　ISBN 1-56280-113-9　16.95

FOR LOVE AND FOR LIFE: INTIMATE PORTRAITS OF LESBIAN COUPLES by Susan Johnson. 224 pp.
　　　　ISBN 1-56280-091-4　14.95

DEVOTION by Mindy Kaplan. 192 pp. See the movie — read the book!　　　　ISBN 1-56280-093-0　10.95

SOMEONE TO WATCH by Jaye Maiman. 272 pp. 4th Robin Miller Mystery.　　　　ISBN 1-56280-095-7　10.95

GREENER THAN GRASS by Jennifer Fulton. 208 pp. A young woman — a stranger in her bed.　　　　ISBN 1-56280-092-2　10.95

TRAVELS WITH DIANA HUNTER by Regine Sands. Erotic lesbian romp. Audio Book (2 cassettes)　　　ISBN 1-56280-107-4　16.95